THE PLASTIC MIGRANT

PROFESSOR RASHID GATRAD, OBE

AND

JADE SMEDLEY-BAUGH

Copyright © 2024 Professor Rashid Gatrad and Jade Smedley-Baugh

The moral right of the authors has been asserted.

Apart from any fair dealing for the purposes of research or private study, or criticism or review, as permitted under the Copyright, Designs and Patents Act 1988, this publication may only be reproduced, stored or transmitted, in any form or by any means, with the prior permission in writing of the publishers, or in the case of reprographic reproduction in accordance with the terms of licences issued by the Copyright Licensing Agency. Enquiries concerning reproduction outside those terms should be sent to the publishers.

This is a work of fiction. Names, characters, businesses, places, events and incidents are either the products of the author's imagination or used in a fictitious manner. Any resemblance to actual persons, living or dead, or actual events is purely coincidental.

Troubador Publishing Ltd
Unit E2 Airfield Business Park,
Harrison Road, Market Harborough,
Leicestershire. LE16 7UL
Tel: 0116 2792299
Email: books@troubador.co.uk
Web: www.troubador.co.uk

ISBN 978 1805145 158

British Library Cataloguing in Publication Data.
A catalogue record for this book is available from the British Library.

Printed and bound in Great Britain by 4edge Limited
Typeset in 11pt Minion Pro by Troubador Publishing Ltd, Leicester, UK

Dedicated to

Sir David Attenborough

Khawaja Mohammed Aslam MBE

and Edna

All proceeds from this book will be donated to Midland International Aid Trust to help the plight of children globally.

It seems to me that the natural world is the greatest source of excitement, visual beauty and intellectual interest – the greatest source of so much that makes life worth living.

– A quotation provided by
Sir David Attenborough for this book

AUTHORS

Professor A R Gatrad OBE DL PhD DSc FRCPCH is a consultant paediatrician at the Manor Hospital and professor of paediatrics at the universities of Kentucky, Birmingham, Wolverhampton and Lahore (Pakistan). He founded WASUP (World Against Single Use Plastic), which is now global and in fifty countries. He has a special qualification in planetary health and is a member of the climate change committee of the Royal College of Paediatrics and Child Health (UK). He is advising the Walsall/Wolverhampton Trust sustainability teams and local councils.

At the age of seventy-seven, he still works in the NHS – now in his fifty-second year. For halving death rates in babies, he was made a Freeman of the Borough of Walsall; for improving access to children into West Midland hospitals, he was awarded an OBE. He has been on various national committees and written over eighty papers in international journals, and two books. He holds three doctorates: Doctor of Medicine, Doctor of Philosophy and Doctor of Science. He holds a National Award for Clinical Excellence.

As CEO to Midland International Aid Trust, he has delivered medical projects and humanitarian aid to over twenty countries. Without his friend and mentor Khawaja Mohammed Aslam, this would not have been possible. In 2014, he was made Deputy Lieutenant to Her Majesty the Queen.

Many of his talks on climate change and his humanitarian work can be found on www.youtube.com/professorgatrad and www.wasupme.com. He has co-authored this political fictional story with Jade to raise awareness of the impact of climate change and plastic pollution globally.

Jade Smedley-Baugh graduated from Liverpool Hope University with a first-class honours degree in drama. She has many years of experience in the amateur performing arts sphere. Following an early career in healthcare, she is now a qualified English and drama teacher and currently holds a post as a school librarian and an academic coach in secondary education. After co-writing and co-directing the stage version of *The Plastic Migrant*, Jade co-authored *The Plastic Migrant*, her debut novella, alongside Professor Rashid Gatrad. A trailer of the play can be viewed on www.youtube.com/watch?v=XHgsWUuJTAc.

PROLOGUE

A political fiction story, *The Plastic Migrant* raises awareness of an impending Armageddon facing our world caused by nature's greatest enemy – man himself. But Manjolo is no such man. His family endured the impacts of plastic pollution and climate change through many generations, without even realising it. Not everyone chooses to see – but, as fortune smiles, Manjolo does…

Can one man be that change?

Let us appreciate and respect what we have, until it becomes what we had. This is something we should never forget. So too is that "No animal could ever be so cruel as man. So artfully and artistically cruel." – Fyodor Dostoevsky

THE SEED

Dover – 2017

"Put your hands in the air where I can see them!"

The din in the shipping container dropped several decibels as a voice, only just audible, broke the deathly silence. Manjolo held his breath, careful not to be the first to alert them to his presence, his lungs clenching alongside his fists. He wondered if this is how it felt to die. Closed in, suffocated and hunted like prey, he wondered if he'd rather die than be another statistic. Another immigrant intercepted at a UK port and bundled like a circus animal into a cage. Sent back to 'wherever he came from' without a penny to his name. The longer he held his breath, the more vivid the thought became.

On the verge of losing consciousness, the container lid was thrown open. Like lava, the sunlight poured in, burning his eyes and bringing him to his senses. Almost automatically, he lifted his muscular arms to his face in defence, only to have them clasped at the wrists and awkwardly manhandled behind his back. Everything about him was powerful, but his once dexterous hands fumbled aimlessly out of sight, while foreign voices became indistinguishable amid the chaos. Around him, men, women and children were packed into the container like sardines, giving him very little room for manoeuvre. Whatever he was saying, it made no difference now. He felt disarmed.

It was over. He'd failed.

Ethiopia – 1992
Wealth and prosperity – life is good.

"Grandpa! Grandpa!"

Manjolo, running as fast as his bare feet could carry him across the burning sand, tried desperately to spot his grandpa somewhere in the vast farm that his family owned, set in hundreds of acres of fertile landscaped land. Behind him ran the Blue Nile, so called because of the sediment it carried. This serpentine joined the White Nile near Khartoum in Sudan, on its way to the Mediterranean to deposit its charge.

The gentle, tranquil trickle of the river was drowned out by his frantic wails. Out of breath and flustered, he spotted his grandpa under a large tree that stood proudly aside the family house. The house was located in the picturesque village of Bahir Dar – a day's journey from Addis Ababa, the capital of Ethiopia.

"Grandpa! Where is Grandma?"

"Manjolo, it's Tuesday. Where is she every Tuesday?"

He sighed, throwing his arms down by his sides in a huff. Rolling his eyes, he muttered, "At the market."

"Yes, at the market. Where else?" his grandpa repeated mockingly, as he ruffled the dark, thick hair on his grandson's downturned head.

Without giving his grandpa any further clue as to what all the fuss was about, Manjolo turned on his heels and ran towards the imminent sunset, through the bountiful fields of corn.

To a small boy, the golden kernels seemed to touch the sky, and as the long emerald blades of grass chorused rhythmically in the light breeze, he ran. He ran as fast as his feet would carry him. It was that time of day. The time to catch the last glimpse of the majestic African sun as its edges kissed the horizon just past reaching distance. That time of day when his youthful eyes would marvel at the reflections of the sun, faceted across the rolling swell of the Nile. That time of day when he ran back to his grandpa and grandma and marvelled at the beauty in front of them.

The lissom body of the Nile perpetually danced its way through many territories with familiarity. Graceful and majestic by nature, the Blue and the White Nile inhabit and bless the banks of eleven countries, bringing with them an economic life source of agriculture, farming and fishing; a cup shared with Mother Nature herself. To Manjolo, it felt like this leviathan force was his, the property of his family and their neighbours, all sharing in its bountiful resources. Its constant flow was euphonious; a reminder that life is constantly moving, constantly dancing around us.

His Nile was idyllic, filled with all the promise of youth. It was a metronome, ever filling the farm with its soothing, infinite current. The optics compressed millions of tiny sapphires into one, as its azure tones leapt and shimmered in the African sun; a nation's wealth encapsulated in its ebb and flow.

And his farm? One of similar wealth and prosperity. A symbol of hard work and just reward; a culmination of generations tending to a turbulent land and learning to live with the whims of Mother Nature. Embracing them when possible, cursing them when crops failed. But wealth was everywhere. Children don't see the ephemeral nature of life itself. Be it their family, their surroundings, their own self. They see infinity. They see the river constantly flowing, never ending, its clean water always providing.

Just as its plethora of golden tones fell into the oncoming dusk, he stood and wondered if it would ever be any less magical, if his older self would still seek wonder in the simplest of places. For now, he just waved.

"Manjolo!" bellowed his grandma from afar. "I'm back!"

But unbeknownst to Manjolo, just a few miles downstream, the banks of the Nile were beginning to paint a different picture – one of death and decay.

The leviathan, though strong, would not always win against nature's greatest enemy – man himself.

Dover – 2017

Manjolo sat, huddled in the back of the police van, vaguely and longingly recalling a time at home. A time that seemed almost a lifetime ago. A world away. At the market with his grandma, when he cried profusely as a livestock van trundled past them. He saw cows, crammed together in the back, their sad eyes peering through the air vents, seeming to meet his and begging him to save them. He cried to his grandma; he cried about how sad the cows were and why evil men must crush them in together like that. Little did he know that this was their last journey. Had he known that at the time, he may have cried even harder. Now he was the livestock, crammed in the back of the van, with sweat and tears and other human excreta, crushed up against the unwashed torsos of men, women and children, looking out with similar sad suffused eyes through the window, waiting for someone to meet their gaze.

The van continued to move on, to an unknown destination, presumably some sort of migrant-processing facility where he would lose what little dignity he had left. He did not know how this process worked. As an educated man, he berated himself for not analysing the ins and outs of travelling to a foreign country illegally, and on a whim, without exploring the potential ramifications of doing so. He bit his bottom lip, harder and harder, until he felt his teeth pierce the soft flesh. Blood seeped into his mouth, the first liquid that had made its way in for hours, maybe even days.

Ethiopia – 1993

Manjolo's father, Nkhole, one of another generation of committed farmers, threw open the farmhouse door and took a proud stride forwards, letter in hand. Forgetting himself and meeting the glance of his mother, he stepped back onto the doormat and shook the dried mud and grass from his feet.

"It's here!" he exclaimed, a wild look in his eyes. "It's here. The reply, it's here!"

Nkhole's mother, Nkhata, hurried to him and grabbed the crumpled white envelope and clasped it to her chest, almost whispering a prayer into the sealed vessel. She handed it back with the delicacy of handling a religious relic. Her son, after hesitating, carefully began to open the seal.

"Wait for your father," Nkhata whispered, as she glanced out of the window to see Manjolo's grandfather, Atupa, traipsing back to the farmhouse, sweaty and exhausted, with a glow from the beating sun on his forehead. As he entered the farmhouse, Nkhole turned to him and proudly held up the envelope. Atupa's eyes met his and they knew it was time – time for change.

Manjolo, hidden behind the doorway to the kitchen, heard their hushed tones and suspected something was up. He crouched down, making himself as small as possible to be privy to the result of the big reveal. He moved his left ear closer to the door, as if this would amplify the hushed sounds coming from the front of the house.

"Manjolo is going to school! My grandson is going to school!"

His grandpa, audibly elated, ran circles around the living room, letter lifted in the air, like a schoolchild let out to break early. He leapt about uncontrollably and jigged his way to the outside for the whole world to know.

No one in their family had ever been to school.

Manjolo's eyes shifted awkwardly. He heard the news, but he didn't mirror his grandpa's joy. He didn't want to go to school. He liked the farm. He liked the sunset. He liked waiting for his grandma to return from the market to show her the insects he had found in the thick groves. He didn't want to do sums and grammar and be an 'educated man'; Manjolo wanted to be a farmer, like his father and his father before him and carry on his farming family name – Ankara.

His grandpa continued his run, out of the front door and into the wide-open expanse outside. His cries of exultation echoed into the falling night. Screams of joy filled the humid air and when the excitement began to tire him, he became still. He cried a single tear. A tear of hope, a tear of joy and, secretly, a tear of sadness for the inevitable end to generations of farming.

Dover – 2017

The van steadied to a halt, manoeuvred and parked somewhere. The back doors were thrown open and a group of officers stood sturdy, ready to receive the inmates. Manjolo couldn't find it within himself to get up; what was the point? What was he getting up for? Stupidly, the officer perceived this as resistance and he was dragged forcibly through the wet wintery mud. Now that his forlorn thoughts were disrupted, his mind careered back into the here and now with some urgency. He was a stranger in a foreign land.

The women and children sailed through to the head of the queue and were taken away by armed guards through a side door. Then, something unthinkable. The same officer brought down his fist forcibly to the right and then the left side of the face of the man in front of him, who struggled to remain upright. Manjolo was confused and anger rose up into his throat – he thought to himself, *And this country preaches human rights?* Then, he remembered Abraham, his headteacher back in Ethiopia, saying, "Whatever you do, do not lose your cool."

Ethiopia – 2005

Manjolo was eighteen now – it was thirteen years since he had started school. Now, another letter, many years after the first – a response to an application, he presumed. It sat unopened in the centre of his small desk, in a tiny room of the hostel where he was boarding. He stared at it, wishing he could make out the words written inside without having to commit to opening it. He was an 'educated man' now. He had learnt all his sums, he had mastered grammar, but he had forgotten how best to plough a field in any weather. He didn't forget the sunrise, though. Every bone in his body remembered it. Long sun-kissed days in the fields, culminating in a bittersweet goodbye until tomorrow. He knew his education was a gift, that he was 'so lucky'. He constantly reminded himself of this fact. He considered himself a pauper in a rich man's house – not being able to do what others did. But he was capable.

He was learned and he had achieved everything his father and his grandfather never could. His next destination was to go to university, or so he hoped. The letter held the answer to his future. But still, a small part of him ached – longed for – the carefree boy he had been. His father and his grandfather led such simple lives with such simple pleasures. He vividly remembered the corners of their mouths raised in awe at the bountiful crop or the desired weather condition conducive to a good yield.

He wanted to hear their voices.

But first the letter. He figured he may as well ring his family with news of some kind; news that would fill them with joy, and him with mixed emotions anticipating what was to come.

He was still that little boy hiding behind the living room wall, waiting to hear the news and what change it might bring. He was still as frightened of the path before him and how far it would lead away from home.

He peeled open the envelope; his eyes skimming the words until:

'We have pleasure in informing…'

***

"Grandpa, it's Manjolo… Grandpa?! The line's awful! Yes. It's me, Manjolo," he marvelled.

"Manjolo?! Ahh, my boy! What news?" was the reply.

"I got in, Grandpa. I am going to university!" He feigned the joy his grandpa needed to hear.

Following the jubilation at the other end of the phone, Manjolo asked, "Where is Father? Can I talk to him?"

A silence followed. Manjolo's mind was racing. A change in the weather, a failed crop, a poor season?

Then, excuses followed.

'He's busy; he's out in the field. I will pass the news on.'

This string of avoided questions created a sense of panic deep inside him. It was like that feeling that you're suddenly falling; your brain seems to burn inside the confines of your skull and for a brief second the world seems to stop. The 'joy' that his grandfather expressed was as feigned as his. Something behind his tone of voice was dark and brooding. Something was wrong.

Dover – 2017

It was a sobering thought, knowing you were so far away from home. Prayer seemed futile. If anyone was listening, they would have heard him long before now. The adrenaline of the last few hours drained Manjolo as he sat in the white-walled, cold, bare cell unable to stay alert a second longer. Finally, he closed his eyes, leading him into a fragmented, disturbed sleep. He dreamed lucidly; he saw his grandpa's face as he waved him off to school on his first day; he felt his grandma's coarse hand, rough from hard labour, grasp his tenderly at sunset. He heard his father's voice, though he couldn't quite make out what he was saying. He saw Raksana, his wife, and the tears in her eyes as he left her, for what could have been the last time.

"Put your hands in the air where I can see them!" bellowed a voice.

A sharp inhalation of breath. He was startled and suddenly awake. Frantic and confused, he glanced around him, searching for the unknown officer barking orders. He was alone; just his own intrusive thoughts broke the silence. Was he dreaming? Or was it a nightmare? In addition to his sense of hopelessness, he had a gnawing feeling in his stomach from thirst and hunger pangs, which were beginning to overwhelm him.

Through the tiny opaque window, he could see the foreign sun setting. It was no longer a sight to behold. A dead moth was decaying on the narrow dusty windowsill. Its wings turning to dust.

ETHIOPIA – 2005

A BBC overseas service bulletin:

> *'Climate extremes in Ethiopia have led to an environmental crisis. Deforestation, over-cultivation of soil and the degradation of natural resources have reared their ugly heads long before anyone was fully aware of their relevance. The once-fertile land, now barren, has*

inevitably succumbed to the pressures its inhabitants are placing upon it. Ravaged by unseasonal colossal rainfalls, alternating with prolonged periods of drought, its people are facing an existential crisis. Wealth and prosperity are a thing of the past, replaced by hunger and famine.'

Manjolo's father, contrary to what Manjolo's grandpa chose to share with him, was a victim. Not a victim of famine or disease, at least not in the classic sense, but a victim of circumstance. His own dire circumstances. The famine had begun in his land; it had stopped providing. The fields had grown dry and arid and the kernels that once reached up beyond the horizon now sagged and disappeared into the undergrowth. The disease was man himself. The pollutants contaminated everything around the farm, microplastics filling the lungs and stomachs of the fish like a tsunami flooding a bay. There was disease and famine. His disease was loss of income; his famine was loss of hope. His outcome was loss of life – his own.

Manjolo's grandpa, Atupa, found him, hanging limply from the tree on the edge of the banks of the Nile. The old man's hands clambered to pull him down, to try and revive life into the motionless corpse of his only son. The water, ceaseless, rolled on past him. The metronome continued to tick, but, for him, time stopped there and then, and never regained the pace or purpose it once had.

Wealth and prosperity – it means nothing in the end.

Dover – 2017

The officer, dictating into a recording device unbeknownst to Manjolo, began his interrogation. "For the record, the date is Monday the 4th of December 2017. This is Officer Nathan Drew, the interviewing officer for Manjolo. Sir, could you pronounce your surname?"

Manjolo's response was an inaudible murmur.

The officer continued, "The gentleman has no representation and is being questioned regarding pending immigration charges. Manjolo, could you please state your full name and date of birth for the tape?"

Still no audible response.

"Manjolo, could you please state your full name and date of birth for the tape?"

Another inaudible murmur.

"Thank you. As you have sourced no legal representation, do you allow me to proceed with my questioning?" yelled the officer.

With a resigned look, a mix of guilt and shame, Manjolo simply responded, "Yes."

"Anything you do say may be given in evidence against you in a court of law."

Manjolo, clearly upset and angered by this remark, said nothing. Nothing was safer than something that would later act against him.

"For the purposes of the tape and the detainee, I will repeat: you are being questioned regarding your immigration status and your reasons for being here. Do I have your permission to proceed?"

"Yes," Manjolo replied, reluctantly.

His response prompted what he could only perceive as a barrage of questions, abuse and interrogative remarks. The walls around him seemed to be closing in on him, his mind wildly playing a string of possible scenarios, like the trailer for a film he had never imagined himself starring in. A criminal detained, interrogated and eventually charged was the only viable outcome he could foresee.

"Who are you and whereabouts have you come from?"

"Who paid for your travel to the UK?"

"Were you asked to conceal, or knowingly carry, any prohibited items into the UK?"

"Which gang are you working for? What are their names?"

"Are you aware that you have broken the law?"

"You do know we are well within our rights to have you face criminal charges and send you back?"

"What you are doing is illegal! What are your true motives for being here? Manjolo, why *are* you here? Manjolo, tell me why you are here."

Vulnerable and overwhelmed, Manjolo summoned it from within himself to respond, not mimicking the arrogance and patronising tone of the officer, but instead with the patience and dignity he had so prided himself on prior to now.

"Sir, please, allow me to tell my story. All of my story. Listen to my reasons, listen to the desperation from which I have fled. Listen, digest it and tell me what you would have done walking a mile in my shoes? Then, if it is still your wish, send me back. I will answer all your questions if you allow me a phone call to my loved ones back home. Just let me tell them I am safe, that's all I ask of you."

Nathan, at the end of his tether, and with his patience dwindling by the second, plagued by the monotony of this type of interview, allowed his humanity a fleeting moment in the sun, "Okay, one phone call. Two minutes."

Manjolo fumbled with the foreign handset. He had used a landline telephone several times in his life, but under the scrutiny of the accompanying officer, he seemed to lose all sense of dexterity and focus. However, with the help of the small yellow sheet affixed to the wall in front of him, he found the international dialling code for Ethiopia. He had no hope of reaching Raksana directly; the only number he could recite by heart was the telephone number of his close friend's business, recalled unintentionally from the catchy jingle that accompanied an advert for a fish bar they aired on local TV some years ago.

The line rang, dull and grainy. No answer, but then someone picked up.

"Catala? Catala? It's me, Manjolo. I'm sorry to call you. I don't know who else to call. I'm alive – tell Raksana I'm alive. I am being held in some sort of a detention centre. I only have two minutes…"

He fumbled, unsure which information was best to relay in a mere two minutes.

"I am trying to find a lawyer, tell her I'm fine. I'm fine. I don't know what will happen next… if they send me back, I'll find her… tell her…"

The line went dead.

He stood for a second trying to recall which information he had managed to share – very little, he feared. He hung the phone back on the wall mount. Childlike and vulnerable, he slumped to the floor, crumpled and broken. Tears ran down his flushed cheeks like the river he had once loved.

Ethiopia – 2005
The crossroads

Manjolo found himself stood at a crossroads. A crossroads between manhood and boyhood; not long plucked from the family farm where he had played as a boy, and not long a student in this fast-paced hive of life, where he found himself now an orphan. He had never grieved for his mother; he had never met her. She had died when he was a tiny bundle in her arms and no amount of delving would ever let him truly remember her. He had never felt that loss; his grandma, Nkhata, mothered him more than enough and his father had been ever-present, making up for what he had lost, keeping him safe with deep love and affection.

Now, just on the brink of manhood, his source of inspiration and revere had been cruelly snatched from him. No, not snatched – that suggested a terminal illness or a cruel accident

– instead ripped, ripped away from him by choice, his father's final choice. His father had chosen his own fate. It was the only thing he could control in the end. The bitterness Manjolo felt towards the man he had always aspired to be curdled inside of him, a cyclone ripping his chest, a turbulence deep in the pit of his stomach, tearing at its very edges.

It seemed he had two choices, two paths running parallel into his horizon. Bitterness, resentment, anger and a shrivelled faith, rendered insignificant by death or happiness. He chose the latter and decided on academia.

At university, he'd made some good friends. He had met Catala and Bambano early in his first year and soon became the nerdy, quiet, academic one of the trio. Catala – funny and good-willed – and Bambano – intelligent, charming and witty – had both unknowingly become his family now. He had his education, something for which someone in his circumstances was to thank the heavens, for it was a blessing wished upon him by his father and his grandfather alike. He just wanted to achieve simple goals, to prove to himself that he could make his father proud. Happiness, it was possible. But still a dark cloud loomed over him. The ceaseless 'what ifs' raced through his mind as he sat absently in a lecture theatre.

The very thoughts of hopelessness that kept him up at night were difficult to silence. What if he had not left the farm? The stupidity of this regret haunted him almost as much as the regret itself. As if his presence could have stopped nature, stopped time and halted the inevitable degradation of an affluent land. Could his single pair of hands have stopped the millions responsible for the catastrophe that his country was suffering? Could he have cut the rope?

Up until now, everything he had ever done had been to make his father proud. He prayed night after night to be a strong enough man to still make him proud in his absence.

Dover – 2017

For a young man brought up on a rural farm, speaking predominantly Amharic, Manjolo's English was commendable. At university, he'd found himself flailing like a fish washed up on the shoreline; he had realised that Amharic was infrequently used and that he had no choice but to seek fluency in a new common tongue – English. However, the exchanges of legal terminology in this police interview and the addition of an alien accent meant that much of what was being said to him was going over his head. The many conversations, consisting mostly of being spoken at, not to, meant that he managed to grasp only the following certainties, or at least that is what he presumed.

Someone had come forward as his legal representative – an immigration lawyer, he presumed. Through some miracle, Catala had managed the near impossible task of convincing the authorities that Manjolo would seek refuge and not be a burden on the country by staying with a friend of a friend.

Then, a realisation dawned on Manjolo. He would have to seek refuge not only for himself, but also his wife – both fleeing poverty and famine. Was a work permit possible? Would the Lord come to his rescue? Would his education help his plight? Too many questions were buzzing in his head, but then came another moment of realisation, which was most terrifying of all. He was being released on bail, pending a trial.

He took out the crumpled piece of paper that had been handed to him by Abraham from his back pocket. "Guard it with your life," he had said. This was all he had, a handful of eleven numbers to contact a man whom he had never met and knew nothing about, but whom he had been sent here to find, to trust. This man was a friend of his old employer Abraham, the headteacher at the school where he had taught back home and a professor at a university somewhere in London, if he recalled correctly. He was Manjolo's intended destination. But

Manjolo was in Dover: alone, penniless, and culturally, bodily and mentally shattered and exhausted.

Would faith rescue him? He often thought to himself that if only he had not abandoned the Lord, things would be different. He had drifted away from his regular communications and, of his own volition, become an island. Even an island needs a life source; a river, an ocean, a stream – anything to feed the growth of what it sustains. Now, more than ever in his life, Manjolo needed divine inspiration – a divine intervention. He bowed his head to pray, struggling for words, not iterating himself anywhere near as fluently as he could when his faith was strong.

After many minutes, he could only manage: "Lord, help me, for I am so lost."

Ethiopia – 2009

On the day of his father's funeral, almost four years ago, Manjolo had recited the following words: "I promise to make him proud, make my grandparents proud and, most importantly, make myself proud." This was a promise he had repeated to himself through the darkest of hours, the longest of nights and the loneliest of summers spent studying in his dorm room, instead of visiting the farm that his heart so yearned for. These last two years would have broken most men.

Following the collapse of the family farm, there had been no hope of it being purchased – not as a farm anyway. The soil had been arid, the banks of the Nile desecrated and the life and soul of the very earth beneath it strangled. The land had fallen to rack and ruin. His beloved grandmother, Nkhata, who had a chronic liver condition, had died of a short illness; gastroenteritis, they had said, contracted through drinking polluted river water. This meant that his grandfather, Atupa, still mourning the loss of his son, Nkhole, only had a grandson many, many miles away left in this world. But then he too had died of an illness, not a palpable one, but a definite illness all the same. The cliché 'he died of a broken heart' had never rung quite so true. He had died of a lack of will to live in the vast emptiness that was once his life. He had gone to bed one night and never woke up. It was not until many days later, when Manjolo's calls had been ringing out, that he had managed to contact a neighbouring farmer who, after gaining entry into his house, had found Atupa tucked up in his bed, Bible in hand, dead. Many days dead.

Manjolo, granted a leave of absence from his studies, had gone home for the funeral. A simple affair with just several of his old friends and acquaintances and no living family member there. He had left Raksana, his partner, behind. Manjolo had, by chance, come across this pretty, charismatic chemistry student, a couple of years older than him, whom he regularly met for lunch and study sessions. She had unknowingly provided a light in his ever-darkening existence. She had offered to accompany him to the funeral, but he had declined, not wanting her to see him weep for the last remaining generation of his family. He had placed an aloe plant on his grandfather's grave, as was the custom, and realised that now there remained no further ties to the Ankara family.

He was an island, at least for now.

But islands grow and change; they adapt to inclement weather and the forces of Mother Nature. They evolve and weather the storm, even against all odds. And this, from some inner strength bred from generations of fighting against the natural order to survive and thrive, is what he had to do.

Manjolo graduated from Addis Ababa University with a first-class honours degree in organic chemistry. He walked tall across the stage to receive his certificate, cheered on by Raksana, Catala and Bambano – now the only family he had.

He was inundated with offers of research projects into various disciplines, including scholarships to further study the impacts of natural and unnatural occurrences on our planetary landscapes.

He was even headhunted by petrochemical companies to spearhead research into methods of making fossil fuel extraction cheaper for them. Would his conscience allow him to do this when the whole world was crying out against drilling oil? He would regularly tune into TV channels and witness how and why the world was getting hotter and extrapolated this information onto the devastating impact around him. He often thought to himself that someone, somewhere, should do something to incite change, and that someone, somewhere, must have the means to tackle what was fast becoming an inevitable fate for the planet.

When he was offered a scholarship to study for a master's degree through 'distance learning', leading to a PhD in green engineering, he accepted unreservedly. He moved back home, able to complete his degree from the place he longed to be. This was just a few miles south of the now dilapidated farm, with Raksana, whom he chose to build his life with. He utilised what little money his grandpa had left him and the money made from selling his farm – and his soul with it – and turned the land, once a smallholding, into a small chemical workshop.

He and Raksana then opened a small school in the adjoining rooms, giving opportunity to village children and adults alike to be educated if they so wished, but in return they had to bring any plastic litter they found on their long commutes to help his research. All this was a small act of defiance against the degradation of his home. A humble affair, with a questionable future, but something that was his, theirs, a future worth fighting for.

Dover – 2017

The room was dingy and crowded with desperate men with anxious faces. As much as he tried, Manjolo could not form any form of relationship with any officers responsible for his containment. They were crude and intimidating, cursing, and laughing at the many foreigners bundled into their holding pens. Except for one. A young woman, who visually recoiled at their racist remarks and seemed to wince when they tried to mockingly mimic the accents of the men, women and children fighting for their very right to exist.

He had seen her holding the hands of women crying through the night, and smile and bob her tongue out at children huddled in fear. She reassured the men, terrified for the welfare of their families, held like captive animals several cells further down the corridor. He had only exchanged a couple of words with her. Lindsey, they called her.

He prided himself on being a good judge of character and recognised her compassion, which was so at odds with her fellow officers. Her short, brown elfin haircut, though giving her a masculine edge, made her look younger, almost vulnerable among the hordes of big, foul-mouthed male officers. Her slight hands regularly fumbled with the keys and she was constantly pushing her navy-rimmed glasses back up to the top of her thin, pointed nose.

Manjolo thought to himself all the time that she did not belong there. She belonged somewhere with humanity. But on reflection, perhaps she was the only slither of humanity there, the fibre holding together the circus of fraught performers and aggressive trainers. He did not believe in the notion of guardian angels – he believed in very little at present – but he did believe that people entered your life for a reason. He believed Officer Lindsay Dean was there for a reason. She allowed herself a sheepish grin.

THE PRIMARY GROWTH

Ethiopia – early 2010

It was the day after Manjolo's wedding in early January.

A humble and simple affair, but one containing more beauty and love than he had ever known. The children at the school had made the couple beautiful cards with equally beautiful wishes inside them; simple crayon drawings depicting love and joy. They had laughed and cheered as the pair had left the evening before the wedding and shared their elation for the forthcoming union of their two favourite teachers.

The ceremony, quaint and tender, went off without a hitch. Raksana, a picture of elegance, reminded Manjolo just how much joy and beauty there was still in the world. The blithe smile of his bride as she stood opposite him was something he would remember forever. Filled with a sudden sense of wanderlust, he wanted to take this beautiful woman and show her all the wonders the world had to offer; show her more than the acrid banks of the Nile and the dried-up soil bordering it. He wanted to travel and seek the joy he felt right now every day of his life. For the first time in his life, he longed to be far from home, whisking his bride off her feet in some faraway land, smelling of exotic scents and oozing wonder and curiosity.

Big plans for an uncertain future.

An air of nostalgia, no longer laced with a bittersweet resentment for life's cruelty, filled his soul as they stood together watching their first sunset. As the intense, harmonious hues leapt across the horizon, he squinted at the blazing glow descending behind the very edge of the world. He held her hand tightly, like he used to hold the hand of his grandmother, and wished with every cell in his body that his family was here to see that he had made them proud.

The air was warm and filled with promise and in that moment Manjolo realised that home was not a thing crafted from bricks and mortar. It was not even the family that nurtured and raised you. In fact, home was not a thing at all. Home was a feeling, a palpable sense of belonging and safety, one of loving and being loved in return – an innate feeling of affinity with whatever it is you chose to surround yourself with. Home had been the farm with halcyon days that conjured up evocative images of his past. Now, home was her and a fortunate situation that he was so blessed to find himself in. He looked intently at the woman who would one day be the mother of his children. He found an almost sublime sense of wonder in her.

He was home.

Dover – 2017

Ordered to pack what little he had, and ready himself for release, Manjolo felt the pang of blind panic in his stomach. He knew he had a very short time frame in which to speak to Lindsay, his possible saviour, and that he was also risking her being berated at the hands of the stern and seemingly rude officers she worked alongside. He needed two things from her; he needed to use a phone to contact Ahmad, the gentleman in London securing his fate, and he needed her to direct him to a church, any church.

Now, more than ever, he needed to test his faith; to solidify the notion that he was placing himself in the hands of God, seeing as the hands of man seemed to do little but desecrate everything they touched.

Manjolo, during his religious upbringing, had often heard the notion, 'the Lord works in mysterious ways' – and, quite frankly, as he stood signing his bail papers, he was really struggling to unravel what path the Lord was willing him to take.

Then, he caught her eye.

She was filing some papers behind the armoured glass at the reception desk. She smiled quizzically, one of recognition and disquiet. For the first time in many days, he felt seen and acknowledged as the human being that he was. He held her gaze and pleaded to her with his eyes. He signalled his head, slightly to the left, where the reinforced door to the back of the foyer was. She winced at him, confused at his poorly executed facial gestures. In the meantime, as the officer handling his paperwork looked down momentarily to sign the bail papers, he frantically pointed at the door.

"You can go," stated the officer, bluntly.

"Nathan, I need to speak to him before he goes," Lindsay half shouted from her position behind him.

Nathan, a short, unsightly man, who exuded arrogance and a prominent stomach, crafted by beer and ready salted crisps, shrugged and continued with his paperwork. His prisoners meant little or nothing to him; what difference would it make to his day if someone else decided to acknowledge their existence?

She made her way to the door, grabbed Manjolo by the elbow and, with a sideways glance, led him down the corridor to an empty interview room. Her sense of unease was palpable.

"You have two minutes," she stated, in an almost authoritarian tone, glancing hurriedly around the room as if someone could hear them.

Manjolo, as succinctly as possible, attempted to cram a lifetime into just a short anecdote, relaying only the necessary facts. A farm, many deaths, a school, a wife, a crisis and his arrival in the UK. He explained that Ahmad, the gentleman in London, knew of his arrival and was providing him with legal representation and that at no point had he meant to break the law. He was supposed to arrive, be collected, make it to London and have everything done legally and above board. He admitted his foolishness in this scenario and fully understood that his own naivety was why he was in the situation he found himself in.

He explained that Ahmad had secured him board and lodgings and that his intention was for his wife to join him, legally, as a refugee. This, none of this, was ever his intention. He himself had been checked and was fertile, but it appeared that, to his dismay, it was his wife who was not. His sole purpose in coming to the UK was to find out why his wife was infertile and what, if anything, could be done. He also wanted to earn some money, legally, and eventually return to Ethiopia. Finally, he informed Lindsay that he desperately needed to use a phone to contact Ahmad and also arrange his accommodation – and that, before any of this, he needed directions to the nearest church.

"A church?!" Bewilderment washed across her face. This man, ripped from his home, alone and quite frankly utterly lost, above all else, needed a church?

"Manjolo, a man cannot live on faith alone," she stated.

"It seems I have little choice," he replied.

Ethiopia – 2010

The school survived as a self-funding, thriving entity for a short time. Many hundreds of students, children and adults alike, passed through its doors. Some came every day, commuting for miles to seek education and gain knowledge in letters and numbers, geography, the religions and science. Some came a handful of times, grasping at what little knowledge they could absorb in the handful of hours they could snatch away from their extensive working hours spent providing for their families. Some popped in for an hour on the way to collect water for their large families and some would not leave for hours after the day was done, reading the books on the ill-stocked shelves until the pages were ragged and the spines barely held themselves up straight. Then, a thunderbolt! After a few months, the school fell onto hard times.

Miracles very rarely happen. Some believe they do not happen at all. Simply believing in such requires one to accept and welcome a 'higher being'. Manjolo, for a religious man, was scientific and logical and, in his world, miracles did not happen. Wonderful things were a product of circumstance – a solid mix of luck and the right ingredients.

Raksana, however, who was spiritual and attuned to a higher frequency, strongly believed in the presence of miracles for those who sought them and, more importantly, for those who deserved them. Whether a turn of fate, a whim of chance or indeed a miracle, theirs came from an unlikely source. Mere weeks from the closure of the school, as the funds – like the farm they came from – ran dry, Bambano chose to visit Manjolo. Their friendship was a great one, one of those wonderful kinships where one can speak very little and not very often, but retain an admirable human connection. With him, he brought Catala. It was a surprise visit and one that would give him some reprieve.

***

Bambano had always been the most likely among the three to financially find his way. He was intelligent and frugal and despite being from a wealthy family, he did not flaunt his wealth. In the process, he accumulated a strong set of financial nuances ready for his leap into the real world.

However, first, he had to learn a trade – a trade that would make him a lot of money. While graduating, with help from his father, he frequented dumping sites under the cloak of darkness, where discarded plastic, mostly single use, was stored to be incinerated. He often recovered plastic that was still smouldering, still glowing from the burning process, in spite of the toxic fumes regularly choking him. Then, he would fill plastic bottles with 'difficult to recycle' plastic, such as empty crisp packets or chocolate wrappers made from multiple plastics. In the beginning, he crafted a few small dolls' houses for children with these 'plastic bricks'. This pocket money further helped his graduation fees.

After graduating, he used his expertise to pioneer a unique business model; repurposing waste plastic into real, functional bricks made from plastic composites. The future of recycling. Not only was the model airtight and copyrighted, but it also made him an awful lot of money. From a small prototype plant, he built major industrial plants churning out bespoke plastic bricks made from melted plastic mixed with sand. Bambano would visit many institutions that collected plastic and pay obscenely small amounts for the plastic he needed to make his bricks, then sell them at a high margin. It was a very lucrative business, or so it seemed.

Eager to 'pay back', Bambano purchased the school from Manjolo. He pumped funds into the building, the facilities and its staff. After Manjolo declined the role of headteacher – saying, "Class teacher suits me just fine" – he employed an amiable and kind man, Abraham Munshi, to run the school. The students, unable to pay for their education, continued to bring litter to pay their way, but this time they were strongly encouraged, more specifically, to bring plastic bottles found on their commutes.

Catala, although she only stayed a week with Manjolo and Raksana, seemed distant, unsure. Something was amiss, but Manjolo could not pinpoint it in the fleeting time they had together. Now a businesswoman herself, Catala owned a successful fish restaurant on the coast serving the 'freshest of catches' to its highbrow clientele. All crisp white napkins and multiple sets of cutlery; it was a world beyond what Manjolo had ever known, a world that intimidated and belittled him. Catala regularly appeared on his TV screen, advertising 'The Fish Locker'. The catchy jingle – 'the freshest catch, a real showstopper, come and dine at The Fish Locker, call us on…' – often went around and around in Manjolo's head for several days after viewing it.

It seemed the trio were all successful, all finding their way and blossoming in their chosen field. But something did not sit right with Raksana, either. Something about the whole situation seemed too good to be true. She was dubious and unsure in spite of Manjolo's constant reassurances, but deep inside her was an intense sense of doubt and unrest. Something was wrong.

Dover – 2017

"You scum – go back home!"

Spit from a local man landed mere inches from Manjolo's shoe, as he continued his string of expletives long up the deserted road.

Manjolo, momentarily stunned, considered his appearance from the outside. He was clearly a migrant; scruffy clothes, with a large backpack, bursting at the seams, and a vacant look on his face.

Almost automatically, he went to check his watch, quickly realising he had handed it to the trafficker as a final payment. He stood, affixed in his spot, a couple of streets away from the detention centre, where Lindsay had told him to wait.

At that moment, Lindsay swerved the jade-green Toyota around the corner a little too fast and pulled up beside him. She wound down the window and, without making eye contact and glancing around as if she was a fugitive, whispered sharply, "Get in!"

Manjolo yanked open the door, ducked his head and pushed himself in.

Lindsay, unsure of what to say to the man next to her, drove silently and with her eyes on the road for the next several minutes. She pulled up at a small church, with a large, slightly decrepit graveyard spanning out to the front. She told Manjolo she would wait in the car. With a nod of agreement and a smile, he exited.

He walked hesitantly through the crumbling headstones, reading the names etched into them as he passed, acknowledging those who had trod here before him. The church door, towering and wooden, with an ornate brass handle, stood slightly ajar before him. Nerves played pranks with his spine. As he clutched the handle, he felt a sense of panic, like he was entering the house of someone he barely knew. He was. His conversations with the Lord of late had been short and few. He almost felt a pang of guilt inside him, like he had lost contact with an old friend through his own deliberate fault.

He took a deep breath and tentatively entered the church. Ordered rows of aged wooden pews sat to his left and his right and a strong smell of incense and old wood filled his nostrils. The dimly lit altar stood proudly at the end of the aisle, with several ecclesiastical candles lit on pillars. In direct juxtaposition to the panic he had felt initially, a sense of deep calm and belonging now washed over him. A sense of home, a sense of safety.

He opened one of the pew doors, careful not to let its creaking break the silence he was so enjoying, and entered. Sitting down and bowing his head to pray, he found himself crying. But, for the first time in as long as he could remember, these were not tears of sadness, of fear or of loss, but tears of joy. Tears of hope, cried by a man who was now resigned to let the Lord be his guide.

Sat in the safety of the church, his mind began to drift to home. When he was away at university, all he had ever wanted was to be back there, but as he got older, he realised it was not 'home' he longed for. He longed for his childhood, the happiness and safety that being part of a family gave him. Yes, he had always missed the farm, the sunset, the cornfields, the large tree with the rope he would swing on as a boy. But when that rope and that tree and that land had become something much darker and more haunting, it was not the place itself he missed. Carefree days filled with the wonder only the eyes of a child can see. That was what he so longed for.

Then, he grew. He met Raksana and on the day of his wedding made a promise to himself that together they would see the world. But life, it seemed, had other plans. There they were, serving the community by providing education – something they were grateful for and something that would help these poor children escape poverty. They did not enjoy the trimmings of wealth, but that didn't bother them as their wealth came from the happiness they found in each other.

As they got older, Manjolo would often remember the promise he had made to himself and wish that circumstance had been such that he could fulfil it. Never, in his wildest of nightmares, had he thought that his first step onto foreign soil would be like this. Entering as a fugitive and a criminal. Entering it alone, without the woman he loved so dearly. Navigating the industrial, built-up and foreign landscape – that would, if the Lord willed it, be his home – seemed a thought far too terrifying to comprehend.

Risking a spiralling train of thoughts that were leading nowhere, he quickly stood up to exit the church. The irony of the situation was that the only person who felt in any way safe was the woman in the car, who was partly responsible for his detainment. If only he could share his predicament with her.

His next stop was the train station, another first. Lindsay – out of kindness or love for humanity, he would never know which – was paying his fare to London. A brief phone call with Ahmad had confirmed their meeting at the other end.

He promised himself as he left the church that he would one day repay this woman for all the kindness she had shown him. He would never forget how one small act of kindness could alter the course of time and his life with it. The butterfly effect – small things that bring big change.

Lindsay explained how to take the train, patiently and without patronising a grown man. She assured him his ticket was fine. He would not need any more money, he would not miss the train, and she joked that he definitely would not fall onto the tracks. As they waited on the platform, she softly reached for his hand, giving it a brief squeeze of reassurance as the train pulled into platform 4. Then, she left. Captivated by the cacophony of sound as the train pulled in, and listening intently to the Tannoy, he realised she had slipped away before he had had the chance to thank her. He was alone now, again ready to step into the next stage of his long and arduous journey into the unknown.

Ethiopia – 2012

Raksana, it seemed, was always right.

Bambano, having appeared in the local press as the 'saviour of the village school' had gained much thanks and praise from the local community. His factory had created many jobs for the local men and women and his 'conservationist' method of recycling plastic into bricks had made national news. He had become quite the local celebrity and a big shot – a *Bwana*.

What he had chosen to omit was that the sites melting down the plastic were releasing toxic and acrid fumes, and that the destitute men working there for him for pittance out of sheer desperation were dropping like flies hovering above putrefied air. He, too, was a regular visitor to the site and Manjolo had, on several occasions, questioned that dull rattle deep in his chest. Raksana, ever the optimist but always a realist, had also questioned this.

It was also a sad fact that the fish inhabiting the once resourceful Nile were now filled to the brim with microplastics and the more they ingested, the more they felt they needed to eat. Starvation and suffocation from within gradually dwindled their numbers. It was also depressing to note that the enthusiastic children who collected their waste on the way to school to trade for an education – while helping to conserve the inches of land they picked it up from – were also conserving the pockets of a greedy and narcissistic man; a man hiding behind the mask of someone who cared for the conservation of a once-pleasant land. For every bottle they handed in, another was burned and melted down in a plant that was suffocating its employees from within. Then, a newsflash:

'Local philanthropist and businessman Bwana Bambano Chiromo dies of a lung condition.'

Manjolo realised that he had lost his friend, the *Bwana*, long before this, when he had found out about the web of deceit spun around his act of kindness and generosity. He could not cry for Bambano, not the Bambano that died that day anyway; he cried for the one he had known many years ago, the man who was clever enough and brave enough to really make a difference in the world, not the one hell-bent on increasing his already lucrative fortune. What Manjolo struggled with the most was that, deep inside him, he felt that Bambano had received his just reward – that he had got what was coming to him and that perhaps his God was not one that forgave but one that punished. Was his father punished, too?

He reflected. For everything he was given, something else seemed to be taken away. In the last year, he had not prayed as he used to – to be thankful and grateful every night – and he had not regularly attended church since he was a teenager. Now, alone in the dark, he could not think of a single thing to be thankful for, except her, because had he listened to her and valued her opinion enough, they would not be in this position. Thinking back to their last meeting, almost two years ago, he had since spoken to Catala only a few times. Bambano's absence of mind and lack of interest in his business during his visit had perturbed him greatly at the time. Yes, he was constantly coughing – why did he not warn him again that it was the fumes from plastic doing this? In hindsight, he had known something was wrong, but his elation at the resurrection of the school had clouded his judgement. He knew one thing for sure, Catala had known all along.

Catala, hearing the news of Bambano's death, felt a weight lift from her heavy shoulders. The secret that Bambano had shared with her all that time ago would be buried with him. Bambano didn't just save the school that summer, he invested a great deal of money into Catala's fish restaurant too, and had helped her with the media and advertising needed to get her clientele back. Bambano knew a lot of important people because he was an important person – a *Bwana* in the local language. The trade and working conditions of employees were kept a secret, but had been questioned by a newspaper reporter: "You are getting plastic from burning sites, which is killing your employees with fumes – have you anything to say?"

The trade, his dignity and his integrity for the business he had worked so hard to build were all washed away as he took his last breath, and they died with him. He died alone, unmarried and without the respect of those who he had once called friends.

As for Catala, there came a stark reckoning. There was a shortage of fish in the Nile and a strong rumour that most fish had ingested plastic that was potentially harmful to humans. Her customers deserted her and she, too, fell on hard times. There was no support from her husband, not anymore.

She had met Friton when he frequented her restaurant, always to see her, then fell in love with him and later married him. But, like so many people she had known over the years, he, too, had been diagnosed with an immune deficiency, and after frequent infections developed septicaemia from his pneumonia and lost his fight for life. He was her rock and the creative one in the marriage, always innovative when it came to business. She was widowed after only a year of marriage and, with losing her husband, she also lost her inspiration and fight.

London – 2017

Manjolo stared vacantly out of the carriage window, following the raindrops with his eyes as they tumbled down the smeared pane. The countryside appeared hazy and mottled outside, the green of the trees smudging into the grey clouds overhead as the train sped by.

Soon, the rolling green fields disappeared entirely and the view was made up of towering grey structures; an industrial landscape alien to Manjolo, with factory smoke obscuring the skyline. Row after row of residential streets appeared one after the other, like one of those books where you flick hastily from one page to the next to create an animation with its pages. Rain-spattered cobbled streets became commonplace and as he approached the city centre, he could only see little over a hundred metres in front of him, as monstrous stone buildings with hundreds of tiny windows standing in lines blocked his view.

People moved here at a pace, like tiny insects. He could see droves of people running around the London train station platforms, scrambling for their train or simply seeking shelter from the downpour. As the train started to slow down to a creep, he was shaken back into the here and now, ripped away from the stories he was constructing in his mind about this foreign landscape that had been speedily painted before his eyes. Panic set in. An inability to move from his seat swept over him and suddenly the fear, anguish and dread of the last few weeks seemed to engulf him like a wave to the shore.

The train laboriously ground to a halt; its inner workings creaking and scraping as the carriage met the platform.

King's Cross Station.

A deep breath in and he stood ready to exit the train, only to be swept up by a sea of people. He was almost carried along the platform into the main body of the station by the crowd, seemingly marching in autonomy.

He steadied himself and, wide-eyed, glared into the vastness of this metropolitan station. The beating pulse of the city cascaded inside of him and his eyes darted from one direction to the other, unable to decide what his next move was. Hundreds of commuters, briefcases or suitcases in hand, scurried around him, almost like a choreographed troupe of dancers, each dancing a solo that criss-crossed the path of those around them.

Ethiopia – 2012

Raksana wept with inconsolable despair for everything that she had lost, everything that was so suddenly and uncaringly ripped from her grasp. Without Bambano's support, the school had closed its doors for the final time and with it closed the book on a chapter of their life that had felt like an endless summer. The sun, the warmth and the comfort on their backs and the promise of a new growth inside of her had deserted her.

The summer ended with such abruptness that Raksana was thrust into a sense of mourning. She mourned for the children no longer able to seek an education in exchange for plastic salvaged on the way to school, and the adults attempting to better themselves, avidly in search of man's greatest asset – education. She was filled with a bitterness and resentment that she had never experienced before, a rising tide of anguish towards not only Bambano and his inexcusable acts, but everything around and inside of her.

Those schoolchildren were hers for eight hours a day; small minds that she could nurture and harness, the tenderness of youth filling her workdays with joy and laughter. She was constantly reminding them of how to respect the environment, to refuse, reduce, reuse and recycle plastic. It was their future that was in jeopardy now.

At home, she had no children. Since the day they had married, her one, all-encompassing wish was to be the mother of Manjolo's child; to build him a new family from the ruins of the one he had lost. It seemed that no amount of wishing or praying in the world could make it happen. No matter how much she begged the Lord and cursed her own internal failures, it would never be enough. She would never be a mother. She regularly repeated this phrase over and over again. She shouted it within the walls of her mind, letting it echo like a whisper in a church, allowing it to reverberate from the edges of the structures she had built around her. Hot, salty tears flowed like the rolling Nile from her darkened eyes, with shadows underneath them – a visual reminder that sleep seemed a thing of the past.

A few weeks after school closure, she returned to the abandoned schoolhouse. Letting herself in, she found herself overcome by every emotion that the last few weeks had conjured up inside of her. She picked up the children's books, still open to the last pieces of work they had been completing, and threw them against the wall, ripping their spines and desecrating what little was left of their education. She was in a frenzy.

She stopped, regaining some composure, and, with her back against the display boards she had so lovingly crafted, she sank to the ground, clutching her knees like a frightened child. In that moment, she realised how little control she seemed to have over herself now. She was faced with the fact that life had broken her and what was left of her heart ached now knowing how Manjolo had felt so many times before. She – the tower and strength and composure – had crumbled from her very foundations; debris now fell all around her as she grasped for what was left. Perhaps she didn't deserve a child of her own; perhaps someone with this much anger inside of them wasn't worthy of bringing a life into the world.

Now, it seemed, she was the one stood at the crossroads. Jobless, childless and unable to face whatever the next day would bring, she sat there, slumped against the wall, for several hours, contemplating what could have been.

Manjolo, concerned for her safety, eventually found her there, lying in the ruins, sleeping soundly for the first time in several days. He held her with the tenderness of a mother holding her newborn for the first time and wiped her eyes with his grubby shirt. He masked his own sadness with the smile she so needed to see and, as dusk fell, they returned home hand in hand, silently acknowledging each other's shared pain. A burden carried by two lighter than that carried alone.

London – 2017

There was a raft of cars, trucks and red buses everywhere, with the smell of diesel hanging in the air. Ahmad was standing on the steps of the station, close to its exit doors, holding a crudely written sign with Manjolo's name on it. Overcome by relief, Manjolo ran towards him and threw his arms around the stranger – perhaps an angel, here to save him. Ahmad, shocked by the embrace, dropped the paper sign and returned the embrace, whispering among the chaos, "You're safe now."

Manjolo would later struggle to recall the hours that followed; a haze of new sights and sounds, unfamiliarity and an innate sense of relief and hope. As the taxi sped away, Manjolo witnessed roads full of big, expensive cars bellowing out toxic fumes from their exhausts with pedestrians on pavements, some with face masks and others ducking into their scarves. A constant reminder of men like Bambano – thoughtless people polluting our planet.

The traffic was heavy but flowing. It was Ahmad who broke the silence, as the wipers started their rhythmic thump to and fro. "We don't know where we are with the weather these days. Even the Met Office can't keep up with the changing weather patterns. This is an unseasonal torrent."

The taxi journey was spent telling Ahmad of the perils he had faced to get here. A non-sensical monologue of despair and hopelessness, his wife's infertility and unemployment. Deaths, marriages and good things that eventually turned bad. A mephitic river, an abandoned farm and a life that had rewritten every chapter that had been so meticulously planned beforehand.

Ahmad, aside from his medical career as a professor, owned a small restaurant. Despite its old, chequered tablecloths and slightly sticky floors, it had been a successful and lucrative side business for many years. His exotic delights excited the palates of many Londoners and he had been able to use the business as a means to help those seeking refuge, offering a bed and employment for refugees.

His main role was that of a senior doctor in the National Health Service and the letters behind his name seemingly formed their own alphabet. He informed Manjolo of the stark reality of his wife's condition.

The fish.

She had, unknowingly, and like many other pescatarians, ingested microplastics to an extent that it had left her infertile. He reassured him that all was not lost and that he knew a world-renowned fertility specialist, a Professor Winston and his team, at Imperial College.

Eighty-six per cent of the fish in the Nile contained microplastic. He termed it a crisis, but one that was widely being ignored in favour of more lucrative and profitable ventures. Manjolo's disbelief was evident; how could the river, once a source of life, become the very thing that was stopping it from forming? Finally, Doctor Ahmad Ali had pieced together a puzzle that, given the facts, would have been so easy to complete sooner. Apparently, the local medical association in Ethiopia was not aware of this, and the so-called fertility doctors he and Raksana had frequented certainly had no clue either.

Manjolo recalled all the times they had visited Catala and eaten in her fish restaurant, all the times that Raksana had insisted that fish was better for humans than meat. Had he been the man he was a month ago, he would have been overcome with regret and resentment, but now, at least, he had some hope. Whatever the future here in London would bring, it would be a step in the right direction compared to the life they were leaving behind.

Aside from the need for somewhere to sleep, Manjolo's primary concern was establishing a legal way to stay in the country and, more importantly, plan a safe passage for Raksana. Ahmad assured him that all of this was in hand and that, as a man of his word, he would do all in his power to save what little Manjolo had left in the world.

The following evening, cold rain pouring from a dismal London sky, Manjolo worked his first shift, washing dishes in a kitchen. From a teacher with a PhD in organic chemistry to a pot-washer in a small African restaurant housing refugees; his now menial work symbolised his descent from 'riches to rags' in only a matter of years.

Most men would feel as though they had left their dignity in the home they had fled, but Manjolo, ever the perfectionist, took pride in everything he did – even this. He would work as hard as he needed to work to gain his work permit, and his wife with it. His hands, fleshy and wrinkled from the hot water and cleaning agents, worked with all the dexterity of a craftsmen, crafting a new life in a new country, pot by pot.

Ethiopia – 2016

Despite the school paying very little, Manjolo and Raksana had been able to save some money by initially living in the extension of the schoolhouse during their time as teachers. But with properties owned by Bambano being repossessed, alongside the rest of his assets, they were rendered homeless. However, their savings allowed them to rent a small room nearby for a short time, but, in their current unemployed state, they were living there on borrowed time.

Manjolo sat counting on his fingers like the children he had once taught. He estimated that they had enough money to last seventeen days in their current abode.

Seventeen days to rebuild a life.

The economic climate mirrored the weather outside – turbulent and unstable. Very few jobs were left in the region, due to the impact of floods, droughts, over-farming, overuse of fertilisers, and pesticides polluting and damaging the once-fertile soil. Many farms were lost and all that remained were business signages on dirt roads, standing like ghosts guarding their former haunts.

Miracle or not, through all the turbulent times, he had completed his PhD by burning the midnight oil, but to no avail as there were no jobs in his chosen subject. People, it seemed, were only interested in making money; planetary health was not a priority for most. With their combined qualifications, they could easily gain a place lecturing in one of the bigger city universities, but, with little money left, they were unable to afford the journeys to get there, let alone secure a fixed abode or even the clothes suitable for interview.

They had spent their lives, up until now, preaching the importance of education and yet, sat there in the dark, just a candle flickering, it did not seem to mean much. For the first time, Manjolo considered it a blessing that God had not granted them a child. What world was this to bring a child into?

Thirteen days later and knowing they could only afford a mere four days in their rented room, they both took to begging. Leaving their dignity behind, they joined many others under a bridge just outside of town. Amid the misery were lawyers, businessmen and other teachers, all embroiled in the unfairness of life and the shattering of their respective worlds. Educated men and women sharing tips on the best place to beg and the most financially viable corners to stand on.

By the end of the day, with just a handful of change, what little hope Manjolo and Raksana had left was extinguished alongside the remainder of the candle lighting the rented room. Four days later, they were homeless.

Five days later, Manjolo begged not for money, but for help.

LONDON – 2018

Manjolo, with many hours on his hands in between shifts, and prompted by Ahmad's insights into the links between the degradation of the natural world and human consumption, decided that he would once again become a learned man. He spent many an hour in the large, grandiose British Library, the biggest in London, marvelling at the towering shelves of archives and endless scientific resources. He earned just enough to pay the bus fare into central London and became quite the regular visitor. He would always be the last one to leave, sat in the dimmed light, absorbing all he could about climate change, fossil fuels, air pollution, the impact of heat on humans, soil degradation, water eutrophication, microplastic in water, the devastating effect of leached poisons from this plastic bleaching corals and seriously affecting marine life – a phenomenon compounded by the heating up of seas through global warming.

His once active brain, slowly lurching back into gear, would tick along, thinking not only of means of prevention, mitigation and resilience to climate change, but means of innovation to defeat this scourge. He was thinking of how we, as human beings and custodians, have failed our planet.

Overconsumption of our natural resources was man's greed coming back to haunt men – the age of Anthropocene. The air, soil, water and everything that sustains life had an acrid human fingerprint. Our planet was on fire, both metaphorically and in the literal sense, from fires raging around the world creating greenhouses gases, warming our world. The greed of man was threatening the Amazon rainforest, which formed the 'lungs of the world'. The corals on which the entire marine world depends on for existence, lying deep in the bowels of the oceans, were dying. Extinction was threatening biodiversity around us; less butterflies and insects means less pollinators, less seed and subsequently less food. To him, this made no sense. Why were we walking blindfolded into this and leaving it to our future generations to pick up the pieces? Would there be any pieces for them to even pick up?

He concluded that we were awful tenants of this planet, moving in and desecrating the property we lease from Mother

Nature herself. We do not own this world; we merely rent our place in it until it is time for the next tenant to take over the lease. We should be gentle, courteous, clean up after ourselves and, preferably, leave it better than we found it. Instead, it dawned on him, humanity was waging a suicide mission, running our planet's resources into the ground and expecting it to, somehow, continuously pick itself up and recover. Were we moving towards an Armageddon? Had we reached a tipping point – a point of no return? He vowed that, if given the means, he would make a difference, not only to his own set of unfortunate circumstances, but to the lives of many, globally.

Not one to wallow in self-pity, he made it his mission to gain as much knowledge as possible while waiting for Raksana to join him and to cultivate a sense of further resolve through the many books on sustainability he was yet to read. Ushered out, as ever, by the librarian at closing time, he always politely informed her that he would be back the following day. With a smile, she would retort that she was always there for anything he needed and that it was a pleasure having him.

Ethiopia – 2017

In spite of being bundled, like a newborn, in towels, blankets and whatever textiles she could fit in the suitcase that she had once used to travel to and from university, Raksana, although in deep sleep, shivered through the early hours on the concrete bed she had constructed under the bridge. Dreaming, she reached over to her left to grab Manjolo's hand, seeking some small comfort and solace. In the small hours, in the cold light of dawn, she dreamt that this was the stark realisation of their life now. The early rays of sun glimpsed through iron railings and stretched across the desolate bed of a river, long dried out, glinting off shards of broken glass and reminding her that, to her dismay, she was still alive to face another morning in the makeshift camp they had been so brutally thrust into.

In addition to being homeless, which brought her shame, she also felt hopeless. Both of these gave her a deep sense of self-loathing. Hopelessness for her meant that not only had God stopped providing, but that she had also lost her faith among the wreck. A faithless life is a hopeless one and a hopeless one becomes very difficult to even exist in.

She fumbled for his hand, finding only emptiness. Still in her sleep, now a nightmare, she panicked and threw away the makeshift sheets, frantically searching for some sign of him. Her eyes darting around the camp, like a wild animal hearing a poacher's warning, she looked for his silhouette in the distance. Nothing. No one. She gripped her covers, pulled them over her head and screamed into them, playing out every possible scenario. Kidnapped? Why? He was a teacher; he was no use to anyone! Robbed? He had nothing to steal. Arrested? Surely, she would have been taken too. She avoided the most likely explanation, reminding herself that not all men follow in the footsteps of their father. Spiralling into a depth that she would struggle to return from, she was, again, frenzied. Then, someone grabbed her arm.

"Raksana? Sorry to wake you up. Why are you crying?"

Raksana was dragged from a stupor.

London – 2018

After months of an endless cycle of reading, working and sleeping, Manjolo finally received news of home and hope. Ahmad had pulled strings and managed to complete the necessary processes to have Raksana brought to the UK, not legally, but with the hopes of achieving such. Manjolo – knowing that, despite the adversity, he had actually been the lucky one of the two – ached to hold his wife. The longing inside of him had hurt far more than his twelve-hour shifts and had pained him more than the hard floor he slept on.

He now had a bit of money and Ahmad, recognising his education and qualifications, had mentioned the possibility of finding him viable employment to remain in the country for as long as he wanted. Ahmad had finally succeeded. The odds were finally on their side. They could now live in a place where nature, and man's abuse of it, wouldn't rob them of everything they called home.

The next day, like every day before, he visited the library. He read about Charles Keeling, who, in 1958, was the first scientist to confirm the proposition by the Swedish scientist Svante Arrenius (in 1896) that anthropogenic greenhouse gases contributed to global warming. Keeling documented the steadily rising global CO2 levels and designed a curve named after him, which measured the build-up of this gas in the atmosphere. Manjolo also read about how, by 1967, the world's changing climate was modelled for the first time, and researched John Mercer who, in 1968, warned the world that ice caps in the Antarctic were melting. He also learnt that it was in 1985, approximately 150 years after the industrial revolution, that there was an exponential increase of carbon dioxide, the main greenhouse gas that made up over eighty per cent of all greenhouse gases.

So, this gas was the major culprit in warming the world, which had already warmed on average over 1.2°C. He read how scientists agreed that with a rise of a further 3°C, the world would not have civilisation as we know it by the end of the century. Perhaps our anthropogenic era was coming to an end, like the era of the dinosaurs.

He studied the data from space stations tracking global climates since the early 1980s and was horrified to learn that the world was ignoring it at its peril. Manjolo had fled many thousands of miles from the plastic-filled, polluted and mephitic river and country that had a hand in the downfall of everything he once had, but, in that moment, he realised you could not flee the inevitable, be it in Ethiopia or in the UK.

He also made a point of meeting Professor Gatrad OBE, a consultant paediatrician and founder of WASUP (World Against Single Use Plastic) – a global organisation he set up to tackle the scourge of plastic. He was intrigued to learn from www.wasupme.com and www.youtube.com/professorgatrad that even a small organisation can have a massive global impact. Even the British breakfast teabags had microplastic in them, and to his horror he learnt how sun creams containing Oxybenzone, a powerful toxin, poisoned marine animals.

He was now also beginning to understand the impact of microplastic and climate change on humans. Thousands around the world were committing suicide because of crop failures. Microplastic was depressing the immune system; toxic fumes from burning plastic were producing dioxins causing serious lung disease, not to mention his wife's infertility and his grandma's cancer.

All of humanity was heading towards a catastrophe. Hindsight is a wonderful thing in isolation; the human ability to recognise our failings and conclude what we could and should have done better will come too late. Hindsight, across the whole of humanity, will be the only thing we will have left when our resources run dry, our oceans die, and our world completely crumbles beneath our feet. After seeing Sir David Attenborough's *Blue Planet* and his other incredible programmes on the small TV in their shared room, Manjolo decided there and then that he would no longer be a bystander. He needed to be the change – but how?

As a young boy, he would run and play. Endless summer days spent in the ignorance of bliss, but the realisation now dawned on him that his pupils back home were not a product of the same soil as his – they grew, many years later, in a far harsher environment. He recalled days when his pupils, exhausted by their commute, would gasp for water. Students would often suffer with headaches and fatigue, something he now recognised as mild heatstroke, induced by the rising temperatures and our inability, as humans, to cope with them. Concentration often waned, even in the most studious among them, and finally all these things, so insignificant at the time, began to formulate in his mind.

On that perilous boat journey to the UK, Manjolo had met many others also suffering from circumstances far beyond their control, man-made circumstances that were devastating their families and their homelands. The English Channel was choppy, and what should have taken only a few hours seemed a lifetime in an overcrowded dinghy, threatening to submerge every few minutes.

Here he had met a Bangladeshi man, whose vast and plentiful farmland had been washed away because of flooding from rising sea levels. Internally relocating to inland cities filled him and his large family with fear of extortion, trafficking and the sex trade. Therefore, he felt there was no option but to migrate to another country. As the boat bobbed up and down, he saw families, visibly malnourished and gaunt – by-products of regular crop failures caused by heat and loss of pollinators such as bees. He saw the fearful faces of women rendered unable to protect their children and the hopeless faces of men unable to save their homes. To these people, and the many millions he was yet to meet, he promised himself that he would make their voices heard.

His research, and curiosity, led him to seek more information about migration. How many 'climate migrants' really existed? How many people were fleeing the impact of devastation caused by their own species? How many other lives were desecrated by the discarded single-use plastic on habitats and ecosystems?

Manjolo feared he wouldn't be the only, or the last, 'plastic migrant' or even a 'climate migrant'.

On his way home, hungry and in search of some sort of solace following this stark revelation, he popped into the corner shop by his lodgings. The storekeeper, Adeje, was always friendly and welcoming, an immigrant himself. They often chatted about the news and how awful the British weather was.

Ethiopia – 2017

It was Catala. She had come to check how Raksana was. The conversations that followed blurred into one for Raksana. By now, she was fully awake and had come to her senses. She remembered that Manjolo had returned to her during the night with only two hours remaining until the boat left and, under the cloak of dawn, had left for England, armed with only a name, an address and a handful of numbers.

***

Their goodbye was the hardest one he had ever known. In that moment, he held his entire world in his arms, and she felt fragile and weak in his hold, like a china doll, weathered and cracked, its dress torn and faded. Her warm tears soaked into his ragged shirt and her sobs echoed through his mind, causing him to hold his breath, attempting to stifle his own. The tower of strength had well and truly fallen, demolished by the turbulence of simply existing, and his biggest fear was not illegally crossing an ocean, but leaving the shell of his once tenacious wife behind.

He held her hands, her head looking to the floor, tears cascading down her gaunt cheeks. He gently lifted her chin and stared deep into her cloudy eyes. Through salty tears, he smiled – the smile she had so longed to see in previous months – and silently promised her that everything would be okay, somehow. Kissing her tenderly on her forehead, he turned and left, holding his breath so as not to release the animalistic shriek of pain and anguish that he was so bravely holding inside.

She dropped to her knees, bereft, and he heard her sobs for a long time as he walked away, refusing to look back on the wreckage he was leaving behind, refusing *ever* to look back again. There was little worth remembering. She sobbed uncontrollably for the love she had lost and the fear that would consume her every waking moment until she heard of his safe passage. Would she ever see him again?

***

Raksana was relieved to see a friendly face and tightly hugged Catala, grateful that she had come to check on her.

Catala tried to recall her recent conversation with Manjolo, in which he had told her about his journey. How he had gone to meet Mustafa, following a chance conversation with a pleasant gentleman who had, only a couple of years before, been the headteacher at the school. Abraham, like many others, had also hit hard times, but had managed to keep his home. He and Manjolo had talked at length about his situation, the school, Bambano, the missed rent payments and finally the bridge. They had discussed how ephemeral happiness had become in the current climate and how stability seemed a distant dream. Then, Abraham had mentioned something that sparked a chain reaction in Manjolo's mind – an idea so far-fetched and crazy that it almost seemed like he was in some sort of an alternate reality, looking in on himself as he considered his possible fate.

Abraham's words had rung in his ears: "The human traffickers, led by Mustafa down by the river, will take you to England if you have enough money, but they do not expect you to carry anything illegal in your rucksack. They will just take you there; the rest, my friend, is your problem. Here, take his telephone number and guard it with your life."

This chance meeting with an old friend and a conversation leading to an unthinkable option would not leave Manjolo's mind. Abraham knew a man in London, a doctor, who had a safe house for migrants. He employed them in his restaurant in return for finding them a permit or helping with legal aid. A philanthropist, a gentleman, an immigrant himself, someone to be trusted. Ahmad, a total stranger in the UK, could be the one to rebuild his life, if Manjolo was to flee.

Overtaken by some spark of madness birthed from a flicker of hope, Manjolo had found himself at Catala's door. There had been little interaction between them since Bambano's demise. Manjolo knew little of Catala's situation, but had come to suspect that Bambano had also been her saviour – at a cost. Before, Manjolo had been angry and bitter; he had thought Catala to be a liar and a cheat like the man who had funded her business for years. However, after some months, he realised that he and Catala were not that different; they were both desperate people, doing what needed to be done to survive. Catala had also regained her dignity. She had found herself an honest job and was now earning a living, leaving behind her an unsustainable and guilt-ridden past, buried alongside Bambano. However, life and circumstance had got in the way and she and Manjolo had drifted onto their respective sides of the river.

But armed with a burning desire for change, Manjolo had found himself back at the mercy of a friend. Knocking on the door, he had inhaled deeply, poising himself to leave his dignity at the door once more and ask, beg if he had to, his friend for enough money to make it to England.

Later, under the cover of darkness, he had shaken hands with the men he had cursed his whole life – thieves and exploiters taking advantage of people with nothing left. Glancing at his wrist, Mustafa had told him he needed his watch to finalise the deal. His father's watch. Manjolo, filled with shame and heartache, had undone the worn leather strap and handed over the last existing material link to his father, hoping that one day his faith would once again be strong enough to find him in the abyss he had been left in, to talk to him once more and tell him that what he had done that day was right, that it had saved his progeny.

This ended Catala's account. Raksana was grateful to her for providing the background to Manjolo's imminent departure and confirming that he had arrived in England.

London – 2020

Raksana wouldn't iterate for many weeks the unspeakable things she had seen and done on her route to England. A shell of a woman, Manjolo feared she had left her best days behind at the schoolhouse, all those years ago. Thin and gaunt, her once-full figure now limply held the fabrics she wore upon it. They hung like damp old clothes from an aged washing line. The glow and wonder in her eyes had dulled now, lost their childlike awe, and the deep brown eyes that Manjolo so savoured staring into were now shallow openings holding behind them months of pain, anguish and fear. He was a man of faith, at least for now, and knew that one day the glint would return and the fire would reignite, but, in the meantime, he would have to gently handle the kindling, so as not to extinguish the spark.

In the early days of her arrival, he took her to the library to see the centre of the metropolitan city he now called home. He took her to meet his work friends and the kind corner-shop owner, Adeje, who saved him food nearing its expiry date. Longing to share and ease their pain, he took her to wander the grassy expanse of Hyde Park, marvelling at the microcosm of city life it held in its natural fortress.

The shadows under her eyes steadily began to decrease and the grip of her hand on his strengthened as they walked. Her wit and humour would now occasionally seep through and the shell washed up on a foreign shore finally began to feel like one that could once again house life.

He spoke to her at length about his research and informed her that Ahmad was attempting to secure him a post as a researcher at a top university – a role where he could continue to grow his already extensive expertise in green chemical engineering and make the first step to being the change he so needed to be. For the first time in months, perhaps even years, he saw the glow of joy spread across her cheeks and life seemed, at least for today, like something worth living.

On his way home from work later that week, he stopped and stared up past the London night skyline, hoping to see the vast network of stars dancing across the Milky Way, but the polluted air and glaring street lights made it impossible. Then, he suddenly felt a pang of longing for home – for his idyllic Nile. Amid the grey stone and murky footpaths, a part of him, though excited for his new chapter, still missed home; the African sunset, the grassy foothills spreading for miles into the horizon, the clear evenings where he could see all the way to the moon, the natural world that he grew up in seemed so far away. Perhaps one day he would see it again with fresh eyes.

All that mattered right now, in this moment, was that she was here, in all her glory, and that meant, however far away he was from his once-prosperous land, that he was home. She was home.

At night, they often talked into the small hours, filling in the many gaps that had formed between their stories, aligning them again into one consistent narrative. Their story had become one worth sharing for generations to come, if God granted them the opportunity to do so. England, unlike Ethiopia, at least had options. Manjolo, having spoken at length to Ahmad, believed there was still hope for Raksana to bear a child, and with a potential new job on the horizon, one that would pay well, this could potentially lead to an even better future for them. This seemed like an option that held some hope, however small.

Ethiopia – 2020

Catala finally felt a sense of repentance, like the deeds of the past could be eradicated and replaced with the good deeds she had done for her friend, her only friend. Though communication from Manjolo was infrequent, she knew that she had done the best she could by him and that whatever came next, she could hold her head high, knowing she had not let him down again.

She would often wander down to the Nile, picking up plastic litter from its banks, and think about their days at university – innocence and naivety being something she wished she could still hold onto. In her thoughts came the realisation that Manjolo, though always 'the quiet one' was, in fact, one of the strongest men she had ever known, both physically and mentally, and that she was blessed to call him her best friend. Deep down, in her very soul, she knew this man would be something more than the young farmer, in his ill-fitting suit, turning up in a class system so far removed from his own. He would be so much more than the small village teacher, trading education for plastic bottles, or the husband, leaving his wife for a pipe dream of freedom and safety.

This man, a leviathan force, like the Nile he had fled, would overcome adversity at any cost. Catala smiled and silently wished him every blessing that life could bestow. God knows he deserved it.

On her way home, unbeknownst to her as to why, she stopped to visit Bambano's grave. The stone, grand and ornate, stood dishevelled and uncared for, weeds reclaiming it and dust almost covering the name etched into the stone. Catala looked upon it with bitterness and resentment, as anger churned up inside her for the man who had deceived everyone and died as a result of his own actions, leaving behind him a wake of debt and destruction, failed businesses and closed schools. Standing, staring upon the lonely tribute to a man long gone, Catala remembered words shared with her in her youth, 'Carrying a grudge only hurts the person bearing the weight, so to forgive is to drop the load.' She would never mourn Bambano – how could she? She would not mourn the innate human failings that he embodied, but she would mourn for the man himself. To forgive was the bravest and most noble thing she could do now, to let go of the blame and resentment she placed on a corpse, to acknowledge her own failings as a human being and stop blaming those who helped her. She forgave Bambano, for all he did, and simultaneously forgave herself, allowing herself the self-respect to become a woman she could be proud of. She felt that she could now take back control of her own destiny and see if she could become half the person Manjolo had become. As she left, she thought to herself that there were many Bambanos around the world, similarly exploiting the poor and killing them.

London – 2021

Sitting by the fire, Manjolo's jaw dropped and, as his eyes gently closed, his mind wondered. When a seed is planted, it requires many factors to grow and develop. One must water the seed, making sure not to drown it or leave it too long to dry out. The soil must be rich in nutrients, allowing the seedling all the necessary ingredients for growth and strength. It needs light – light in abundance – but also shade if the sun beats down too hard. It needs care, either at the hands of Mother Nature or the hands of a farmer, encouraging it into its primary growth phase, allowing it to develop from a vulnerable shoot to a strong, formidable stem. The stem needs support, something holding it up straight so it can follow the sun's path and continue to grow and change, perhaps a cane holding it steady or more compost sprinkled around its roots.

Shoots will start to form and the plant will start to take its place in the great expanse of nature, providing pollen for worker bees or bearing fruit for its human counterparts. Take away the sunlight or the water or the soil support and the plant will start to droop. Its once sturdy head will hang limp and eventually wither and die. That doesn't mean it can't be saved; nature often finds a way to return it to its once idyllic condition and, more often than not, its abundance will return and find the sun again, turning its face back towards the light.

We, as human beings, are more like plants than we choose to admit. Let us grow in the right conditions, ones filled with care and nurture, and we develop happily, leaning towards the sun. Take those things away and we wilt, downtrodden, until eventually we wither and die. But a wilted plant is not a dead one; it's a plant worth saving, worth giving another chance at the life it deserves. Bambano could not be saved. Catala, though it took time, finally lifted her head back towards the sun. Raksana, though withered and dried up, was placed back into the light, allowing it to be absorbed by every cell in her being. She flourished, with glowing colours attracting love and respect from all around her. Nature's beauty restored; a new seed planted.

"Manjolo, it is past midnight," shouted Raksana.

Suddenly awake, Manjolo realised that his nutrients had depleted and his light had faded, but he had defied the odds. He never wilted, he never faltered, he weathered every storm that life threw at him. His roots, hardened and strengthened by many generations before him, wove deep into the ground, steadying him. Though his leaves flailed in the wind and his stem bent under immense pressure, only briefly did he ever lose sight of the sun. His perennial nature kept him coming back, summer after winter, year after year, until finally he was strong and hardy, able to withstand any rainstorm or drought. He stood strong and proud, among the garden he had planted for himself, a perfect example of Mother Nature's craft, a leviathan force, ready to hold the line and reconnect with his Lord.

'That same day, Jesus went out of the house and sat by the lake. Such large crowds gathered around him that he got into a boat and sat in it, while all the people stood on the shore. Then, he told them many things in parables. A farmer went out to sow his seeds. As he was scattering the seeds, one fell along the path and the birds came and ate it up. Some fell on rocky places, where they did not have much soil, but they still sprang up quickly only to wilt under the heat of the sun. Other seeds fell among thorns, which grew up and choked the plants. Yet more seeds fell on good soil, where a crop was produced — a hundred times what was sown. Whoever has ears, let them hear.'

– Modified from Matthew 13

THE SECONDARY GROWTH

Ahmad worked hard to keep his promise from all those years ago and Manjolo was granted a research post at Cambridge University. He found the first rung on a long and fruitful ladder to success – ten years after he had first set foot into an unknown country.

The Times, 20th March 2030
Global Conference on Planetary Health, O2 Arena, London

> *'Today, Professor Manjolo Ankara gave a talk on how he had expanded research of other scientists into seeding chemical sulphates and iodides – which have a similar structure to ice – into clouds forming "artificial rain". This method helps dissipate the nasty effects of pollution on those cities affected. Ending his presentation, he asked the global audience to "watch this space".*

Raksana, rising to her feet on the front row, applauded her husband, cheering and exuding pride for the man standing at the podium before her. She reacted to every word as if it was his first speech, a maiden voyage into this world so far removed from their own. People around her always reacted in much the same way. He was a brilliant speaker, passionately evoking the need for change.

He now shared his research with globally renowned academics, talking to those who chose to listen, as well as those who didn't, about the negative impacts of climate change and the profound scourge of plastics on our natural world. He had travelled to every corner of the planet, but found most joy and solace when he had returned to the place he had once called home and planted a tree to honour those who had not withstood the test of time, many years ago. He had finally made them proud.

Manjolo's successes by now were many. He was the product of many years of careful sowing and tending and was finally seeing the fruits of his labour. Raksana, too, had borne fruit – a little boy, named Abdi, meaning 'hope' in Amharic – thus completing the final piece of their jigsaw. His pride, in everything they had built for themselves, knew no end and he finally felt like a tenant renting space on this earth who now rightfully deserved his place.

But, despite all his successes, and his platform to incite and ignite change, he hadn't yet been the change. His story was not complete; he still had a few chapters left to write.

London – 2040

Manjolo, now fifty-three years old, sat with a furrowed brow, perusing a research journal at his desk. Abdi, not long home from school, leant over his shoulder, trying to make sense of the complex wording before him. He turned and smiled at his son, his eyes tired from many hours staring at the screen.

"Let's go outside, Abdi."

Feeling a sense of nostalgia, he took his son to walk the many routes he had done as a young migrant; the long, cobbled streets and the small areas of natural beauty he had managed to find in between. He showed him Ahmad's restaurant, where dreams were slowly and steadily built, and talked at length about the library and the quaint, grey-haired, bespectacled librarian who had fed his curiosity for so many years.

Crossing the road, he stopped and smiled, looking towards a small corner shop with a tatty sign. He decided he should meet the man who had so often filled his empty stomach and chatted to him about the weather when no one else had given him the time of day. Holding his breath, he slowly opened the creaking door, hoping he was still alive after all these years. Behind the counter, now in a dishevelled-looking, cheap, vinyl wheelchair, a familiar and friendly face stared back at him. Recognition washed over him, like a ghost from the past had wound up back in his establishment.

Adeje was visibly old and frail, holding onto the last threads of his beloved working life, still at his counter, serving his community. He fidgeted the whole time with his hands in constant rhythmic motion – *a symptom of some neurological condition*, thought Manjolo with sadness. He embraced him and all the years melted away from his face. Wrinkles carved by many years of toil seemed to disintegrate into youth and his mind carried him back to a time over twenty years ago. They talked at length, retracing many years of missed steps, completing chapters with missing lines. For Adbi listening, it was a past he knew very little of, unravelling before him.

With a promise to return, Manjolo hugged him tightly as the shopkeeper handed him a small piece of paper, wishing him good luck and good fortune with it. Thereafter, Manjolo kissed the top of his warm head and left in tears, not wanting to look back, fearing it may be the last time he saw the man he had once called a friend. Glancing down at his hand outside the shop, Manjolo chuckled to himself. A lottery ticket sat in his open palm – this man's final gesture of goodwill, albeit an unlikely gesture of good fortune.

Several days later, going into his wallet for small change for a man on the street, he saw this ticket peeping out at him. Upon his return home, he checked the numbers. He checked them again and again. He had Raksana triple-check them. It seemed he would no longer have to rely on faith alone.

The BBC, ITV and Sky News – 1st August 2047

> 'Originally a migrant from Ethiopia, Professor Sir Manjolo Ankara from Cambridge University has won £980 million – the biggest ever win on the Euro Lottery. The ticket was given to him as a gift by a friend, who has sadly since passed away. The professor has vowed to use his winnings to "make a global change". He has pledged many millions of his fortune towards projects focusing on children's education, mitigating the impacts of climate change and the scourge of single-use plastic worldwide. Sir Manjolo said, "Finally, I have the tools to make a difference to our planet. God has given me this money and I owe it to Him and the world to invest it wisely, in its growth, not its depletion."'

Ethiopia – 2057

Manjolo, unlike many, had managed to navigate life without accumulating much debt, at least financially. Whenever someone had granted him a good deed, he had always vowed to pay it back in return. One thing that had always eaten away at him was the closure of the school in his village back home.

Amid the dry soil and the rolling river, he opened his 'Be the Change School', the first of many globally. God looked down upon the hands that would forge many an education and this man, from such humble beginnings, would finally be able to root many seeds to follow. His curriculum would educate the students on the dangers of microplastics, promote environmentally friendly practices and, most importantly, equip the next generation with the tools they needed to succeed and grow.

On the evening of the grand opening of the school in his village in Ethiopia, while being celebrated by all of those around him, Manjolo snuck off into the grassy banks behind the schoolhouse. He stood watching the glorious sunset, alone with his thoughts, and spoke at length to his father, his grandfather and his grandmother. He told them of all his exploits and how every one of them had been in a bid to bring pride to his family name. He felt their presence around him, felt the warmth of their embraces inside of him and, despite standing alone, in the dark, he felt part of a family again. He felt like he had created a legacy worth passing on.

From this day, Abdi would hear so many stories of love and joy that Manjolo was finally able to share with him without sadness, regret or remorse. He would honour his ancestors, allowing their stories to live on through his own son, allowing their legacies to grow and strengthen, not wither and die like the land that had once taken them.

Forever humble and charitable, his next action with his many millions was to set up an education aid foundation, one where, like his school many years ago, children around the world could trade waste and litter for a much-needed education. As his hard-earned PhD had paved the way to most roads that he had taken, and his influence was finally able to pay off where it was needed most, he set up scholarships for studies into 'global sustainability'.

The Times – 19th September 2060

Ankara Will Save the World

> *'Ethiopian philanthropist and businessman, Professor Sir Manjolo Ankara, now a Nobel laureate and arguably the richest man in the world, has discovered a process more energy-efficient than simply recycling plastic, which has taken industry by storm on a global scale. The conversion of plastic back into oil will not only reduce the pressures*

continually placed on landfills worldwide and decrease pollution, but it will also provide copious amounts of oil to be reused in industry globally until alternative sources of energy have proven to be viable.

The production of plastics, made up of eighty per cent oil, emits eight per cent of greenhouse gases worldwide, as well as having a negative impact on both animals and humans alike. Ankara's model will substantially diminish the contribution made by plastic to the production of greenhouse gases.

His patented methodology is being tapped into by global giants, providing huge employment opportunities: the impacts are such that presently the projected figures showing our disposal of single-use plastic will be reduced by up to seventy per cent in a mere three years. Billions of tons of plastics will be repurposed instead of simply being sent to landfill sites, where it stays for hundreds of years, leaching poisons that affect local soil, habitats, marine and human life.

His son, Professor Abdi Ankara, a graduate of Imperial College, has recently taken over the post at Ankara (Global) Industries as CEO and vows not only to continue his father's pioneering work and that of the company, but also to promote conservation worldwide, planting many millions of trees in areas impacted by widespread deforestation in the Amazon and elsewhere.

Ankara Industries does not only own major shares in engineering factories and industries around the world, but also owns major media conglomerates. Ankara is now the biggest company of its kind in the world, with offices in seventy countries and a turnover of billions. Abdi, while rubbing shoulders with world leaders, has also vowed to continue to support government initiatives to harness wind power to electrolyse water to produce hydrogen for energy, *reducing our need for fossil fuels. In the process, oxygen will be released. A win-win situation amid a global crisis. In addition to his robust business model, Ankara continues to fund and manage the international school project, "Be the Change", where students can trade waste and litter for a "free" education in poorly resourced countries.*

Referring to his dad's idyllic River Nile, Professor Abdi also emphasised that the world's biggest natural resource, drinking water, only forms four per cent of global water and is seriously threatened; therefore, more work is needed to protect it from the increasing stress from plastic and petrochemicals waste, incineration and other sources of pollution. With most plastics made from fossil fuels, it is imperative to address plastics to address the climate crisis and protect our earth and its waters.

With our natural world balancing precariously at a catastrophic tipping point, Abdi hopes that governments on an international scale continue to buy into his business model and encourage research, allowing the change that our natural world is so desperate for.'

Dover – 2068

Philanthropy, conservation and the protection of the natural world had become part of Manjolo's life and that of his family members. By now, working with different governments and local councils, he had set up flood-resilient task forces in many countries vulnerable to floods to educate people about, for example, the planting of mangrove trees along coasts as a defence against floods and setting up early warning systems. His projects to resurrect the Amazon forest were going well.

But as his life careered into old age, his only wish was that his son continue the legacy they had worked so hard to create.

Raksana, now a grandmother, had flourished into old age, the lines on her face mapping a path that led to all the happiness she could ever seek. It was never the money that brought such joy, although most of it was spent bringing joy to others, but the safety that Manjolo brought with him; the courage and the fight that she knew would always keep her protected and loved.

Abdi had grown into a fine man; he saw the world and every marvel in it, and looked at everything with the awe of a child. He was God's greatest blessing upon them and would continue the story that his father had started many years before, adding in page by page, chapter after chapter of great tales.

As Manjolo's story started to wind down to its final chapter, there was one line not yet written. A promise made in the summer of his youth that would be fulfilled in the winter of his life, many miles away.

Upon his return to Dover, he found the church that had saved his faith. It had sadly closed its doors many years previously and its yard was now overgrown, dilapidated and uncared for. To the left of the church was a small wooden bench, dedicated to parishioners long gone, surrounded by overgrown forget-me-nots and weeds. He had arranged to meet her here at noon.

Lindsay, now also in her eighties, looked searchingly for him, wondering if she would recognise a ghost from over fifty years ago, wondering if his smile still resembled that of the terrified young man she had briefly known. To her, their interaction had been small, somewhat insignificant – a forgotten memory long erased. It wasn't until he had got in contact that she considered the profound impact she had had upon this now globally successful man; that she was the catalyst that had turned a dishevelled, hopeless migrant into the inspirational man sat in front of her. He stood up, extending his hand as though to shake hers, but then sandwiched her hand between his and embraced her, holding her delicate frame tightly in his, whispering, "Thank you," into her ear.

Of all the debts he had ever repaid, this was the one that would allow him to die a happy man. To simply acknowledge a small act of kindness that had incited so much, by a woman who unknowingly had saved him that day, was a huge burden finally lifted. Small talk initially was followed by talk of Manjolo's phenomenal journey. Finally, after hours, Lindsay asked if, amid his countless successes, he had any regrets or anything left unfulfilled.

"Yes," he said, "I would have loved to meet Sir David Attenborough, to share an hour or two, to trade stories with the man who, among others who came before him, kept me inspired through those dark, dreary afternoons in the British Library – the man whose documentaries kept me enthralled in those lonely months that now seem a lifetime ago, crackling and fading in and out on the black-and-white TV in the apartment above the restaurant."

She laughed, a sincere and knowing laugh. "I'm sure one day your name will be as widely known as his. Maybe it will one day be *you* who he seeks to meet!"

They continued to chat until the sun fell behind the church walls and the chill in the air crept into the churchyard. But just before embracing him in a tight, lingering hug, she whispered something that Manjolo would remember to his dying day.

"Manjolo, I told you all those years ago that a man cannot live on faith alone. I was so wrong."

POSTSCRIPT

Facts about climate change and plastic pollution that were highlighted in the story.

"Humanity is waging a suicidal war against our planet."
– UN Secretary General

We presently have a global climate crisis at a possible tipping point – a point of no return with temperatures soaring inexorably. To get on track to 2°C rise, a thirty per cent reduction in greenhouse gases is needed, whereas a fifty-five per cent reduction is needed to achieve 1.5°C – our acceptable aim suggested by the Paris Agreement in 2015, signed by 196 nations at COP 21. But the world continues to remain blindfolded.

During the summer of 2022, the record-breaking heat resulted in over 60,000 deaths in Europe alone, and in 2023 we have witnessed the hottest ever recorded global temperatures in Europe, North America and Africa. In China, 53°C was recorded. Then in the same year global temperatures reached 1.63 °C! These extremes of heat are getting more extreme and lasting longer with 'ever burning' fires in many countries endangering life and limb. Some are classing this year as the start of the tipping point. Scientists are now not calling this global warming, but 'global boiling'.

Human health, both mental and physical, is inextricably

linked to the health of the earth's natural systems, which create the air we breathe, the food we eat and the water we drink. This complex set of relationships is sometimes referred to as 'planetary health' and moving forward it is increasingly recognised as a critical perspective for the health of our future generations.

The climate crisis also poses a substantial risk to the healthcare infrastructure and vital services, not forgetting its impact on individual health caused by heatwaves, flooding, wildfires and conflicts leading to a greater demand for hospitalisation. This is already evident, with further pressure from the presence of vector-borne diseases, such as malaria and dengue fever, in areas where they previously did not exist.

Ever since the industrial revolution, over 150 years ago, greenhouse gas emissions have increased, particularly carbon dioxide, and indeed over the last fifty years exponentially so. In addition, human activity has removed over half of wild birds, mammals, fish and insects from our planet. In fact, a global study of 71,000 animal species found that forty-eight per cent are declining. A further pertinent example of our human activities affecting the ecosystem is the staggering figure of one hundred million sharks killed for food per year, decimating their population.

Over the last one hundred years, sea levels have risen 11–16cm and it is estimated that they will rise by 50cm in the next one hundred years as more and more arctic glaciers melt. Many islands, such as the Maldives, will simply sink. In fact, there is an inexplicable phenomenon of 'hazard flips' where areas that were prone to drought now experience flooding and vice versa.

Over 6 billion tons of plastic waste have reached our waters over the last fifty years. As this waste lasts hundreds of years, the original plastic that was manufactured is still on this planet! Only ten per cent of global plastic is recycled. Eight per cent of greenhouse gas emissions are from plastic manufacture, the main fossil fuel in its production being oil.

Our daily consumption of single-use plastic and their composites are filling our oceans; marine life is strangled and strewn across litter-filled beaches, which are becoming a telling sign of humanity's failings. Pollution of our rivers and sea corals, on which all marine life depends, are in a crisis and heading for extinction too. A further sobering thought is that recent studies (2024) have confirmed the presence of microplastics in the human reproductive tract.

The impact of air pollution due to the burning of fossil fuels is greatest on children whose physiology is such that their breathing and heart rates are faster. This results in more toxins being inhaled. Their immature organs, particularly the brain, are more vulnerable to the particulate matter in air pollutants. With pregnant mothers being similarly affected, children are therefore exposed from the womb to the grave.

These <2.5 micron pollutants (particulate matter) in the air, aside from causing breathing problems such as asthma, escape

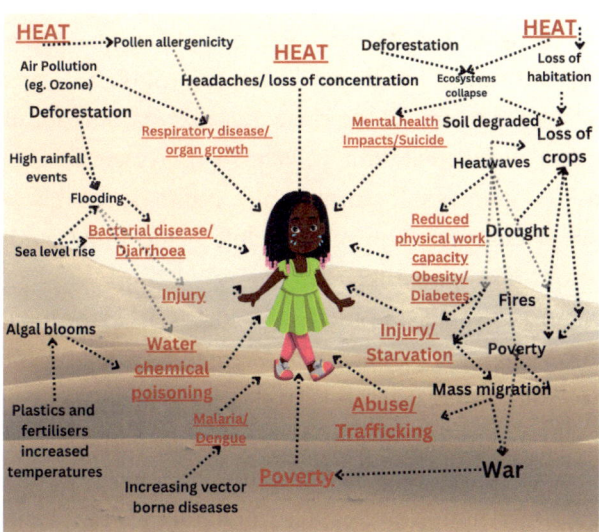

The impact of climate change on a child.

the lungs and impact on every organ of the body, affecting cognitive and other bodily functions. They are implicated in cancers, strokes, heart attacks, dementia and diabetes. According to the WHO, over ninety-five per cent of children globally breathe 'toxic air'.

Children also have a relatively large body surface area per weight, compared to adults. Added to the fact that they also have an immature sweating system makes them more vulnerable to rising temperatures affecting their health, daily activities and concentration in schools. Climate inaction is costing lives and livelihoods today, with new global projections revealing the grave and mounting threat to health of further delayed action on climate change. Bold climate action could offer a lifeline for health. Climate emergency is a health emergency.

Warnings have been issued by scientists for over forty years in response to worldwide concerns regarding soil erosion, depletion of natural resources and habitat loss, made worse by widespread deforestation as a result of mindless actions of farming, timber and mining companies. These warnings are now a reality. If global warming continues to change faster than we can change its course, there will be an Armageddon not in some distant future, but in our lifetime; a frightening prospect for many, but a reality all too close. As custodians of our planet, we have so far failed abysmally. What is more, we are spending billions on space exploration, while millions on this planet continue to starve – a prime example being India landing a lunar probe in August 2023.

Scientists invented the engine that kick-started the industrial revolution and it is scientists, in different ways, who can and will help save our world, but they have to act quickly as there is a global climate emergency and each one of us has a part to play. We can, for example, start by eating locally grown food, decrease our beef consumption and use less fossil fuel-based transport.

Research should be the bedrock of all universities and

institutions, and be supported by government grants and subsidies, be it for harnessing energy from the sun and wind to produce green hydrogen for energy through electrolysis of water, or ways of capturing carbon.

In our present anthropogenic geological era, our innate greed is coming back to haunt us and, in the process, affecting populations of poorly resourced countries with catastrophic effects. An example of this being food insecurity, through droughts, floods and fires affecting millions of children worldwide. According to UNICEF (2023), forty-three million children have been displaced over the last six years in forty-four countries and the United Nations High Commissioner for Refugees António Guterres stated that human-induced climate change will become the biggest driver of population displacement in this century, prompting an estimated 150–200 million people to move by 2050. This climate crisis is so complex that even the physical and mental safety of children is affected during 'climate migration' because of flooding, conflict, crop failures or drought.

Bellizzi et al. (2023) state that although the term 'climate refugees' has been introduced since 1985, in practice those people may not be able to claim asylum based on climate change reasons alone and as a result do not have adequate access to legal protection of their rights.

It is, however, heartening to know that a number of countries (Argentina, Finland, Australia) have started to offer special arrangements in order to protect persons displaced by natural disasters (e.g. visa schemes facilitating moves etc.). They conclude that early preparation and early warning systems are crucial in order to address those situations, alongside collaboration.

Although probably an underestimate, five million deaths a year are directly attributed to fossil fuel use and air pollution globally. Furthermore, it is expected that there will be 250,000 additional deaths per year from undernutrition, malaria, cholera, other diarrhoeal diseases and heat stress. Additionally, there is a global threat to the ever-decreasing ground water supply for sustenance, and direct effects of weather on crops are affecting global food security.

It was in 2020 when residents of ten villages surrounding Lake Baringo in Kenya saw their homes being submerged as lake waters swelled past human habitability. These residents were marginalised in an internally displaced persons' camp and when they were asked what had displaced them, they replied with one simple word, "Water" (extracted from Climate Change eBulletin, August 2023 – Royal College of Paediatrics and Child Health).

Is it not ironic that the more our world develops, the more challenges it faces? To readdress this imbalance, we need to revive our human values, not based on greed and overconsumption, but on learning about and understanding the impact of our activities on the natural world. We should all share this concern to help make our world a safer, more equitable place in which to live. A place where the eight people who control half of the global wealth could dig deep into their conscience and ask themselves, "What can we individually or collectively do to mitigate this climate emergency?"

We must also remember that most countries strive – some, at least, in theory – for their populations to achieve their full potential and be happy. Each country should work in its own way to achieve this and wealthier countries should help the poorly resourced ones to lessen human suffering. This will then inevitably contribute to a much happier world order. In the words of Bill Gates, one should be judged 'on how well you address deepest inequalities, and how you treat a people a world away who have nothing in common with you except their humanity.' A recent example in 2022 was the flooding in Pakistan, a country that only contributes to one per cent of global emissions, yet was, and continues to be, disproportionately affected. Here, there was a fourfold increase of malaria, including in those provinces where it had been completely eradicated.

No religion condones the destruction of our planet indiscriminately; on the contrary, all religions in their own way make us, humans, custodians of this planet to ensure happiness and health.

With shortage of land though fires and floods, man and animal will come closer and compete for food and land. Man will eat unusual animals with transmission of zoonistic viruses such as Covid and Ebola, leading to pandemics possibly worse than Covid.

With the loss of snow and ice over the poles (permafrost), there will potentially be hydrocarbons and viruses that have been buried for centuries released, which man will not be able to cope with. Is this a world we want for our children?

Exercises and workshops for schools

In schools the following can help children appreciate the problem of sustainability, climate change and plastic pollution:

1. Describe how you / your family can make changes to your lifestyle and/or other actions which will result in the reduction of green House gas emissions. (500 words) – run an essay competition.
2. Where are rain forests in the world and name as least 6 ways in which trees help humans, animals and the environment?
3. What type of plastics can be found in the school environment – identify them and discuss which are easy to recycle.
4. Name sources of renewable energy – advantages and disadvantages
5. There is only 4% fresh water globally for human consumption. Think of ways in which you can save water.
6. How can you decrease plastic pollution in schools by using the 4Rs – Refuse – reduce – reuse and recycle?
7. Explore what has brought about climate change – there are 3 good reasons.
8. Explain the greenhouse effect as it affects our planet.
9. Why is climate change man-made?
10. Explore plastics that can be made from non-fossil fuels.

Quiz

1. When did the Industrial revolution start and what is its significance to climate change?
2. Which are the 3 fossil fuels, and which one is worst with respect to greenhouse gases?
3. Which is the most ubiquitous greenhouse gas forming at least 80% of all greenhouse gases?
4. Name other 2 greenhouse gases.
5. Which greenhouse gas is largely released from agriculture?
6. Which greenhouse gas is at least X80 more powerful than carbon dioxide?
7. Ammonium nitrate is the main constituent of particulate matter which pollutes the atmosphere. Which of the two is worse for our body – PM10 or PM2.5 or less?
8. The particulate matter that is worse for our body can seriously harm us. How?
9. Burning of diesel – such as in cars produces a potent polluting gas – which one is it?
10. Burning petrol and diesel are both bad – which is worse for the environment?
11. If there were no bees our food production around the world would be affected. Why?
12. Trees can help produce rain as happens in the Amazon. How?
13. What is plastic made from?
14. If we don't control plastic production there will be more plastic (by weight) in the oceans than fish by 20….
15. How long does plastic take to disintegrate?

Answers to the Quiz

1. Over 150 years ago. Since then there has been exponential increase in greenhouse gases from the burning of fossil fuels.
2. Coal, gas and oil. Coal is the worst
3. Carbon dioxide.
4. Methane and oxides of nitrogen
5. Methane e.g. cows burping and passing wind!!
6. Methane
7. PM2.5 microns or less – can travel for thousands of miles and is the biggest culprit
8. PM <2.5 microns not only affect our lungs givin us asthma and cancers, but it penetrates through our lungs into our brain (causing dementia and strokes), our heart (causing heart attacks), our pancreas (causing diabetes) and it also causing cancers in other parts of the body.
9. Nitrogen dioxide.
10. Diesel.
11. Population of bees and other pollinators are declining because of human activity and climate change. Bees pollinate and produce seeds. Seeds produce our food.
12. Trees go through a process of transpiration creating rain. Many countries surrounding the Amazon Forest rely on this rain.
13. Largely from oil and gas
14. 2050
15. Hundreds of years

A Poem

By Patricia Hughes – Chief WASUP Ambassador – Liverpool (UK)

The world we want

Last night whilst in bed
beautiful images came into my head.
Mountains so majestically high
Reaching up to a starlit sky.

Then birds sang sweetly to let me know
that sunlight was creating a golden glow.
In dense forests with trees so green
animals climbing and swinging were seen.

Lakes and rivers so clear and bright
beautiful creatures, oh what a sight.
In fields bloomed bright coloured flowers
where children played for many hours.

Oh, what a beautiful sight
why only seen in my dream at night?
Now wide awake I want all this to stay
so read this book and share it today.

REVIEWS

A tale, intricately evocative, one that weaved a thread of devastation leading to resilience. With incredible facts, this book contains immense knowledge in every alphabet. I am inspired to fight with an even greater resolve to save our planet.
– *Lubainah Majid: Chief Youth Kashmir and International WASUP ambassador. Climate and Justice Activist.*

The story tugs at our heart strings. You simply want to know what happens next. I just could not put it down. A wonderful, thought-provoking book for adults and children alike to read, enjoy and help make a difference to our world. The stark reality of the planet we are living in is laid bare in real time, not only in this fast-moving story but also in the fantastic scholarly overview by Professor Gatrad in the postscript. Exercises and a quiz at the end are a perfect way of engaging us all. The book ends with a beautiful poem which will motivate us to work towards a world we want. I would highly recommend it – a must read.
– *Paul Ingles, Head Teacher Cooper and Jordan primary school Aldridge, Walsall*

Professor Gatrad has crafted a story that is both timely and timeless, reminding us of the enduring power of kindness and the critical importance of environmental stewardship. Through Manjolo's journey, the book challenges us to ask whether one person can indeed be the change the world so desperately needs. A must read.
– *Eshal Shaukat: Chief youth Pan Asia and International WASUP Ambassador, Pakistan*

ACKNOWLEDGEMENTS

We would like to thank various people who helped with the production of this book – in particular, Gemma Spittle and Valerie Gatrad.

A special thanks to Paul Ingles for his tireless effort and inspiration in bringing to life the stage version of this book.

The authors would also like to thank the Midland International Aid Trust, in particular Mohammed Aslam MBE, for supporting this project through WASUP (World Against Single Use Plastic).

www.wasupme.com
www.youtube.com/user/professorgatrad
www.miatwalsall.org.uk